SCHOOL OF FEAR

BY
GITTY DANESHVARI

ILLUSTRATED BY
CARRIE GIFFORD

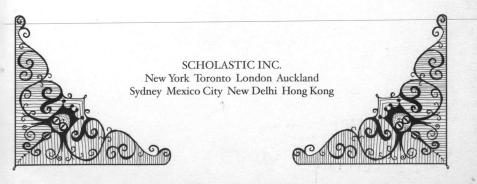

SCHOLASTIC INC.
New York Toronto London Auckland
Sydney Mexico City New Delhi Hong Kong

For Shamsi

This edition published by arrangement with Little, Brown and Company, New York, New York, USA. All rights reserved.

ISBN 978-0-545-28440-0

Text copyright © 2009 by Cat on a Leash, Inc.
Illustrations copyright © 2009 by Carrie Gifford. All rights reserved.
Published by Scholastic Inc., 557 Broadway, New York, NY 10012, by arrangement with Little, Brown Books for Young Readers, a division of Hachette Book Group, Inc. SCHOLASTIC and associated logos are trademarks and/or registered trademarks of Scholastic Inc.

12 11 10 9 8 7 6 5 4 3 2 1   10 11 12 13 14 15/0

Printed in the U.S.A.   40

First Scholastic printing, September 2010

Book design by David Caplan

SCHOOL OF FEAR

The wilderness outside Farmington, Massachusetts
(Exact location withheld for security purposes)
Direct all correspondence to: PO Box 333, Farmington, MA 01201

Dear Applicant,

I am pleased to inform you of your acceptance to the summer course at School of Fear. As you already know, School of Fear is an exceedingly select institution, run by the elusive Mrs. Wellington, aimed at eradicating children's fears through unorthodox methods. The small group of parents, doctors, alumni, and teachers aware of our existence vigilantly maintain our anonymity. It is at the discretion of this small group that students are referred. We strongly advise all incoming applicants and their families only to discuss School of Fear in the confines of their home with the television on, water running, and dog barking.

On behalf of Mrs. Wellington and the entire School of Fear staff, I would like to welcome you.

Warm regards,

Dictated but not read
LEONARD MUNCHAUSER
Lead Counsel to Mrs. Wellington and School of Fear
Munchauser and Son Law Firm

LM/kd

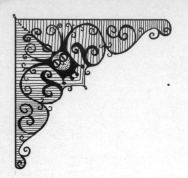

EVERYONE'S AFRAID OF SOMETHING:

Mottephobia is the fear

of moths.

A bell is not a bell. While undeniably constructed out of metal and heralded for its ability to ring, it is actually a great deal more than that. It's the taste of barbecue, the feel of sunburned skin from playing outside all day, and the smell of chlorine from freshly cleaned pools. It's the promise of football games, sleepovers, and video-game tournaments, all without the interruption of homework. In short, the bell is the gatekeeper of summer.

At Brunswick School for Girls in the posh Kensington neighborhood of London, a group of twenty uniformed students waited for the final proclamation that the school year was over. With desperation brimming in their eyes, the girls watched the clock and waited for the bell. A chorus of petite navy blue shoes, rife with impatience, banged against weathered chairs muting the teacher's voice.

Disregarding the teacher was hardly a new trick, but on this particular day, the girls did it with the deft ability of guards at Buckingham Palace, the fuzzy hat–clad group who refuse to react under any circumstance. With mounting frustration, the girls wondered if the bell had gone on holiday. It had a history of doing that during exams, oral reports, and other academic nuisances.

Thoughts of mischief frolicked through nineteen of the twenty girls' minds; however, in the back of the class, there was one young girl determined to will the bell *not* to ring. Raven-haired Madeleine Masterson had purposefully chosen her seat for its obstructed view of both the clock and the bell. Madeleine's blue eyes darted rapidly as she repeated three simple words, "do not ring," under her breath. For the first time in her short life, she had nothing but trepidation and fright for the start of summer.

Normally Madeleine savored summer's many quiet afternoons spent in the drawing room with a book, puzzle, or Internet-equipped laptop. Madeleine prided herself on having an above-average understanding of world politics. Most students did not know the name of Norway's prime minister, Jens Stoltenberg, but Madeleine did. She also knew, and more impressively could pronounce, the names of Greenland's Prime Minister Hans Enoksen, Iceland's Prime Minister Jóhanna Sigurdardóttir, Mauritania's President Mohamed Ould Abdey Aziz, Benin's President Yayi Boni, and so on. Madeleine staunchly believed that all of the one hundred ninety-two member states represented at the United Nations deserved to be studied.

Madeleine would gladly spend the summer at Brunswick School for Girls if it meant eclipsing her parents' plan for her. She would live off the drinking fountain and vending machine; she simply needed to make sure she had enough coins. The idea began to take shape; Madeleine could ravage the library, devouring books by the armful, skip through the halls, and sleep in the immaculate infirmary. A summer at Brunswick would be utterly delightful!

Regrettably, Madeleine's plea to stop the bell was flatly denied at exactly 3:00 PM. The piercing sound rang through the grand halls of Brunswick, inciting a stampede of girls in sharp navy-and-white uniforms. Much like the running of the bulls in Pamplona, the rush to leave school was a dangerous event. Luckily, this wasn't an issue for twelve-year-old Madeleine. She had long insisted on waiting ten minutes for the children, nannies, and parents to clear the front of the school before leaving her chair.

On that particular day, Madeleine was so drowning in dread that she lingered in the classroom for an extra forty-five minutes before exiting. She mentally alphabetized the list of United Nations delegates as a means to pass the time. Madeleine knew her mother and the driver were waiting; however, she had to summon the courage to face summer. It is a rather lamentable fact that few can call upon courage with the expediency they can fear. And Madeleine was no exception.

Mrs. Masterson, keenly attuned to her daughter, had

expected the delay and brought the *Herald Tribune* to read. Fortunately, she found the plush interior of her chauffeured Range Rover far more relaxing than the couch in her drawing room. After reading every pertinent story, Mrs. Masterson flipped the newspaper over just in time to see Madeleine nearing Brunswick's Victorian-styled main gate. She exited the car as Madeleine emerged from the shadows wearing a netted veil and a belt of aerosol cans. The young girl wildly sprayed the air around her while speeding toward her mother.

"Hello, darling, how was school?"

"Very well, Mummy, thank you for asking. May I inquire whether the car has been fumigated today?"

"Of course, Maddie."

"I do hope you're not fibbing, Mummy. I can tell the difference. My nose is quite discriminating."

"Fibbing? That is ludicrous. I assure you the car has been thoroughly fumigated today."

"Thank you, Mummy. Aren't you going to ask why I am late?"

"No, darling."

"Very well, then. Now, if you don't mind, I would very

much appreciate a quarrel and subsequent grounding. Perhaps one that lasted the entire summer, or if necessary, even longer."

"Don't be afraid, Maddie; it's going to be like camp," Mrs. Masterson said cheerfully.

"I've been to the cinema, Mummy! Camps have poorly insulated cabins with spiders, millipedes, and cockroaches that will climb all over me. I can't possibly spend the summer in such squalor!"

Madeleine's intense and obsessive fear of spiders, insects, or bugs of any kind greatly distressed her parents. It was an all-consuming fear that affected every aspect of her life from school to sleep. In the evenings, Madeleine prayed for a spider-free night before climbing beneath a canopy of thick mosquito netting. Already shy by nature, Madeleine had a fear of spiders and bugs that created an additional barrier for her to conquer socially.

Madeleine often remained at home, unwilling to stay in any structure that hadn't been fumigated recently by exterminators. The brightly colored stripes of an exterminator's tent gave her the warmth and excitement that most children reserved for birthday or holiday gifts. Regrettably, few parents at Brunswick were willing to meet the costly and time-consuming demands of the young girl behind the netted veil.

In an effort to pinpoint the exact origin of Madeleine's fear, the Mastersons racked their brains for traumatic incidents involving spiders or bugs. They came up empty every time. As early as Madeleine's first birthday, they remember her crying fervently at the sight of a daddy-longlegs spider. With time, Madeleine's fear became more hysterical and extreme, until the Mastersons could no longer rationalize it as a normal childhood stage.

At six years of age, Madeleine drove herself into a panic-stricken state, complete with heart palpitations, after she watched a grasshopper slip through the front door. She became obsessed with the idea of the musically inclined creature crawling across her face while she slept. The mere thought made the already weak-stomached girl keel over with nausea. Within minutes, Madeleine gave her parents an ultimatum: move or call Wilbur, the trusty exterminator.

Wilbur had spent so many nights at the Masterson household that he not only was on their speed dial, but he also received holiday cards from them. He was an extended member of the family and the only person in the world who actually relished Madeleine's fear. If it wasn't for Madeleine, it was doubtful he would have been able to afford annual holidays to Bora Bora. So when the Mastersons called about the grasshopper, he happily obliged. It was an awfully expensive job to remove one measly grasshopper, but Madeleine insisted.

In front of Brunswick School for Girls, Madeleine prepared to enter the car when a shiver crawled up her spine. Instinctively, she grabbed her repellent and prepared to spray.

"Don't shoot!" a shocked classmate begged, hands above her head in the surrendering position.

"Sorry, Samantha, I wasn't sure what was behind me," Madeleine replied as she lowered the can.

"When was the last time a spider tapped you on the shoulder? Honestly, Madeleine," Samantha said with exasperation. "I'm having a party tomorrow afternoon and I thought you might like to come."

"Would you mind terribly having it at my house?"

"I beg your pardon?"

"The party. May we do it at my house?"

"Then everyone will think it's *your* party."

"I suppose that's true. Has your house been fumigated lately?"

"Sorry, Mum says she won't fumigate again. Can you at least stop by for pizza?"

"I'm sorry, but I don't think it would be prudent. Plus, your mum doesn't much like the smell of bug repellent."

Mrs. Masterson listened to the exchange with a sinking heart. She only hoped that after the summer Madeleine's "problem" would cease to exist. As intelligent, polite, and soft-spoken as Madeleine was, she was equally dramatic where spiders or insects were concerned. Mrs. Masterson had been forced to confront Madeleine's issue several months ago when she requested a note to excuse her from physical education class at school.

"Mummy, please write a letter informing Mrs. Anderson of my inability to play outside due to the flesh-eating virus I recently contracted."

"The virus isn't a problem indoors? Just outside?" Mrs. Masterson asked with amusement.

"Mummy, the virus feeds off the UV rays of the sun."

"Surely you don't have to choose such an extreme

disease to avoid playing outside. How about something simple like a cold? I don't want the school calling the Center for Disease Control again."

"Mummy, must you bring that up? I had no idea that foot-and-mouth disease was real. I was put on the spot and it popped into my head."

"Flesh-eating viruses are real too, Maddie."

"Yes, Mummy, but Mrs. Anderson has given me no choice in the matter. She said that short of a flesh-eating virus I would have to play outdoors."

"Maddie, don't you think it would be easier to play outside?"

"Mummy, not to be cheeky, but I would truly rather have a flesh-eating virus than go outside."

Mr. and Mrs. Masterson had tried traditional therapy and hypnotism to quell Madeleine's growing fears, but both were fruitless. The therapist and hypnotist believed Madeleine's dread of spiders had morphed into a phobia, arachnophobia. Of course labeling the fear did little to alleviate it. When instructed by Mrs. Anderson to attend school without her veil or aerosol cans, Madeleine faked her own kidnapping.

An hour after discovering the ransom note in the kitchen, Mrs. Masterson found Madeleine cocooned in mosquito netting at the bottom of her closet.

"Madeleine, what are you doing down there?"

"Mummy, I've been kidnapped; do you mind coming back later?"

"Darling? Who exactly kidnapped you?"

"No one was around, so I had to kidnap myself."

Mrs. Masterson nodded before asking, "Any reason in particular for the kidnapping?"

"That mad, bonkers Mrs. Anderson is forcing me to go to school without my veil or repellents. It's cruel and unusual punishment. I think I ought to consult a solicitor," Madeleine said.

"Honestly, darling, there isn't a solicitor in England who would take your case. On the off chance that you were *seriously* planning on taking legal action."

"Mummy, I don't have time to discuss this; I've been kidnapped."

"If I speak to Mrs. Anderson and convince her to let you keep your veil and repellents, will you call off the kidnapping?"

"Well, I suppose so. But you'll still have to pay the ransom. It's five quid."

"I don't have it on me, but I can get it from your father downstairs. Will you come out in good faith?"

Shortly after the great kidnapping scare, Madeleine's school counselor, Mrs. Kleiner, invited Mr. and Mrs. Masterson to her office for a private meeting. Mrs. Kleiner's office did not come equipped with a comfortable couch, as Mr. Masterson had predicted, but rather two very uncomfortable baroque chairs. Mrs. Kleiner closed the office door, locked it, and pushed a towel against the base of it. Mrs. Masterson had only ever seen someone do that when there was a fire, as a means of blocking the smoke. As Mrs. Masterson prepared to ask if there was a reason for the towel, Mrs. Kleiner flipped on the radio. The gray-haired counselor removed her oval glasses and dabbed the sweat off her upper lip before speaking.

"Thank you so much for coming in today. I have an important story to share with you," Mrs. Kleiner said quietly.

"We're delighted that you've taken an interest in Maddie," Mrs. Masterson responded.

Mrs. Kleiner nervously nodded before beginning her

story. "About twenty years ago I enrolled my niece, Eugenia, in an atypical program after she became petrified of dogs. If she even saw a dog, she would faint straightaway. She could be in the middle of the road, and boom; Eugenia would be facedown on the asphalt with black cabs and lorries barreling toward her. And all because there was a little white poodle a mile down the road."

"How frightful," Mrs. Masterson exclaimed.

"I've never much cared for poodles," Mr. Masterson said absentmindedly.

Both women chose to ignore his comment and continue with the conversation at hand.

"We needed something potent for Eugenia's phobia, yet with a proven track record, which isn't an easy combination to find. However, after much research, that's exactly what we found."

"I'm so pleased to hear that. What is it called?" Mrs. Masterson asked.

Mrs. Kleiner looked both ways and then whispered, "School . . . of . . . Fear."

"School of *what*?" Mr. Masterson asked.

"Shhhh. You mustn't throw that name around. You cannot tell anyone what I am about to share with you. It is of the utmost importance that the details of the program remain vague to allow students the highest possible chance at recovery."

"Mrs. Kleiner, is this a school or Scotland Yard?" Mr. Masterson asked jokingly.

"Mr. Masterson, this is a school unlike any other and as such requires total discretion. Are you both prepared to make that sacrifice for Madeleine?" Mrs. Kleiner asked sternly. "Because if you aren't, I shall turn off the radio, remove the towel under the door, and stop whispering. I am late for a game of backgammon as it is. If you're not serious about helping Madeleine, tell me now."

"Of course, we are very serious about helping our daughter," Mrs. Masterson responded while staring down her husband. "I can't tell you how concerned we are for her lungs alone. All that repellent can't be good. She wakes up three to five times a night for maintenance sprays."

"Are you absolutely sure you can handle it?" Mrs. Kleiner asked while staring coldly into their eyes.

"We're sure," the Mastersons responded.

Mrs. Kleiner explained that School of Fear is an exceedingly exclusive program run by the elusive Mrs.

Wellington; it is actually so select that few people are even aware of its existence. If one asks a postman, greengrocer, operator, or judge about School of Fear, they won't have a clue. The general public has no idea that such a place exists because the chosen group of parents, doctors, and teachers in the know are vigilant about maintaining the institution's anonymity. It is at the group's discretion that candidates are nominated, as Mrs. Wellington requires a letter of personal recommendation to consider a student.

Continuing with School of Fear's clandestine nature, rigorous background checks are performed on both candidates and their families. These background checks are so thorough that Mrs. Wellington often learns information that belies logic: everything from eating paste in preschool to misspelling one's own surname in second grade.

After acquiring all pertinent information on the applicant and family, Mrs. Wellington then requests an essay of no less than one thousand words detailing the child's fears and the traditional methods that have failed them. Points are deducted for grammatical errors, spelling mistakes, and poor penmanship. The application explicitly states that all essays are to be handwritten, as Mrs. Wellington doesn't care for dubious technologies such as typewriters and computers.

Not since the Mastersons changed health-care plans had they heard of a process with so much red tape. There was fingerprinting and extensive tests with peculiar names such as The Standardized Childhood Insanity Exam and Personality Defect Assessment. Overall, finishing the elaborate application was quite a feat considering it was all handled through the mail. Mrs. Wellington did not wish to disclose the identity of her employees prior to acceptance. While the candidates may have been in the dark about Mrs. Wellington, her private investigators ensured that nothing escaped her attention.

If Mrs. Wellington was notified of an information leak during the application process, candidates were immediately disqualified and sent a stern warning from her private attorney at Munchauser and Son. As anyone could tell you, no one messed with Munchauser Senior, absolutely no one. Many former students became fixtures in society while never breathing a word of their days at School of Fear. It was a two-part vow of silence, one for extreme loyalty to Mrs. Wellington and the other for fear of the infamous Munchauser wrath.

Leonard Munchauser Senior was known for his wicked temper, ruthless nature, and cold heart; and that was with his family. The story goes that he once removed his son's eyebrows, one hair at a time, as punishment for spilling milk. Worst of all, Leonard Munchauser Junior's eyebrows were permanently affected, growing in spottily and lopsided. As atrocious as that may have been, it paled in comparison to the treacherous tactics Munchauser Senior employed to protect his clients. And no client was of greater importance than Mrs. Wellington and School of Fear.

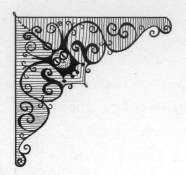

CHAPTER 2

EVERYONE'S AFRAID OF SOMETHING:

Phasmophobia is the fear

of ghosts.

W hat do you mean Grandma's dead? How could you let this happen?" Theodore Bartholomew howled in the kitchen of his family's messy Manhattan apartment. The stout boy with alabaster skin, dark brown hair, and milk chocolate eyes framed by glasses stared at his mother in shock.

"Grandma was old, that's what happens. Old people eventually die," Theo's mother, Mrs. Daphne

Bartholomew, explained compassionately, placing her hand on top of Theo's.

"But you're old. Look at all those wrinkles. You'll be dead soon too!"

"I'm not *that* old."

"All I see are liver spots and wrinkles," Theo said as he started to hyperventilate. "I feel faint — quick, get the smelling salts!"

"I can't remember! Where do you keep those?" Mrs. Bartholomew asked with exasperation.

"Must I do *everything* myself?"

Theo pulled a first-aid kit from his jacket, grabbed a white stick, and snapped it under his nose. Even from a few feet away Mrs. Bartholomew felt the effects of the pungent smelling salts.

"Sweetie, are you okay?" Mrs. Bartholomew asked softly.

"My grandmother's dead, my mother's on the way out, and I just used my last smelling salt," Theo droned.

Twelve-year-old Theo was the youngest of seven children, and by far the most, well, everything. That was the thing about Theo; he was rather hard to describe since he was so many things. He was definitely the most dra-

matic, hysterical, and neurotic boy in the bor
Manhattan. He was also kind, genuine, sweetly
and a vault of unusual facts. His mind often journe
to dark places, setting off a hailstorm of concern, which
he didn't think twice about sharing.

Oddly, Theo's siblings never worried much about
anything other than getting into the bathroom first.
Therefore, it was hardly a surprise when Theo took his
grandmother's death the hardest of all the children.
While admittedly a tad insensitive, his siblings were
grateful for the extra space their grandmother's death
provided. Before judging the Bartholomew children,
one ought to remember that Manhattan apartments are
unbelievably short on space, prompting many landlords
to list closets as bedrooms.

Regardless of the rationale, the Bartholomew children's
interest in their grandmother's room offended Theo. He
thought it best for the room to be kept as a shrine to his
grandmother, complete with her hearing aid, dentures,
and heart medicine. Her stuff was the last vestige of her
presence in his life, and moving it felt downright sacrile-
gious. The shrine idea, along with the "We Miss Grandma"
tee shirts, were vetoed at a Bartholomew family meeting.

Theo's disappointment in his siblings intensified when none of his six brothers and sisters joined him in throwing their bodies on the coffin at the funeral. In true Theo fashion, he considered the act to be a testament to loyalty and love. As Mr. Bartholomew spoke at Morristown Cemetery, Theo stared at the oak coffin covered in white lilies. His father's voice echoed in Theo's ears as he ran full-speed toward the casket, ultimately knocking off the lilies. He held on to the coffin tightly, his face squashed against the smooth wood. Theo believed that if he had died first, his grandma would have done the same for him. He saw it as one final hug, albeit through a casket.

With tears streaming under his glasses, down his soft skin, and onto his snug suit, Theo felt a hand on his back. It was his older brother, Joaquin, sent to fetch him. Theo released his grip, allowing his brother to lead him back to his seat. Theo's dramatic performance continued with him squawking "Why?" loudly while looking at the sky.

"Because she was ninety-five," Joaquin calmly responded.

Theo glared at his brother, irritated by his literal response.

"What? Was that a rhetorical question?" Joaquin just didn't get it.

Shortly after Theo's grandmother's funeral, the already anxiety-prone boy developed an even more intense fear of death and a fanatical need to track his family's whereabouts. Theo demanded hourly contact with each member of the family to confirm that they were alive. All data was logged into a notebook aptly labeled, "Dead or Alive." It was quite a striking title, but Theo did have a flair for melodrama.

Sitting in his family's dark living room, the walls lined with books and paintings, Theo opened "Dead or Alive" and began with his eldest sister, Nancy. He had last seen her running out the front door with only a cardigan to keep warm. Theo worried she could catch a cold, lower her immune system, contract meningitis, and contaminate the whole family. He had prudently texted her to get a jacket, surgical mask, and some antibacterial hand sanitizer, but she ignored him. As he dialed her number, Theo shook his head, thinking about how often his siblings thumbed safety in the face.

"Nancy, this is your brother . . ." He paused, expecting

her to greet him warmly. "I suppose since you have four brothers I should identify myself by name. It's Theo."

"Trust me, I know who this is, Theo," Nancy said with obvious annoyance.

"Good to hear," he replied with an oblivious smile. "I need verification of your safety and well-being. And I wanted to encourage you to return home to get a heavy coat, surgical mask, and hand sanitizer."

"Stop calling me, I'm on a date!" Nancy fumed.

"I'll take that as an affirmative that you are alive and well. And make sure your date washes his hands before holding yours — lots of germs going around this time of year. Okay, have fun. I'll call you back in an hour."

"Don't you dare!" Nancy yelled, but Theo had already hung up the phone.

Not even the strict rule against cell phones at school stopped Theo from checking on his family. He constructed a system during school hours in which each family member was required to text Theo a confirmation of his or her status, alive or dead. It wasn't necessarily the most logical system, since a dead person can't text. In fact, Joaquin and his two other brothers often texted back "dead" as a joke.

Theo never laughed. Even with his elaborate and time-consuming system, thoughts of death continued to plague him. His siblings started referring to him as Theo the Thanatophobe — thanatophobia being a fear of death or dying. Theo didn't acknowledge the name, feeling justified in his behavior after reading the newspapers' accounts of death from car accidents, sickness, crime, and other grotesque manners.

Theo's neuroses were never quite as heightened as when his parents went camping in Yosemite National Forest in Northern California. Between the remains of ancient glaciers and towering redwoods, there was absolutely no cell reception, preventing them from checking in. Theo's imagination went into overdrive as he envisioned grizzly bears devouring his beloved parents.

Without consulting his siblings, Theo decided it was downright irresponsible of him not to do as much as possible to safeguard his mom and dad. He figured if they couldn't check in with him, he would check in with them, by any means necessary. Various accounts of his parents being injured, attacked, trapped by fires, or lost were reported to park rangers.

"I said *lost*! What part of *lost* do you not understand? They asked me to get help!" Theo screeched.

"If they don't have a cell phone, how did they tell you they're lost?" the ranger smartly asked.

"I have the gift. . . ."

"Of bull," the ranger added.

"The psychic gift. PBS is doing a special on me in the fall," Theo lied. "Please, you must find them!"

"Listen, kid, I wasted eight hours yesterday with that phony fire story. I'm not falling for this again."

After the park rangers threatened legal action against Theo, the Bartholomews realized it was time to get help. Since they both were theology professors at Columbia University, they decided their first course of action would be to inquire with other faculty members. They waded through a few boorish comments about military school and fat camp until they found a psychology professor whose son had overcome a fear of foreign languages at a private institution in New England. Apparently, the fear had been so pronounced the boy refused to go in public without headphones. Of course, before the professor told the Bartholomews the name of the institution, he looked both ways down the hallway and closed his office door. Like others in the know, the professor chose to whisper when speaking about School of Fear.

The Bartholomews salivated at the notion of eradicating Theo's thanatophobia and other general anxieties. Of their seven children, Theo was by far the most time-consuming and draining with his constant worry. Mr. and Mrs. Bartholomew asked their other children to stay in their rooms while they spoke with Theo. Seated on a maroon loveseat, his parents explained their plans for his summer at School of Fear.

"Are you out of your mind? *School of Fear* sounds like a cult! Why not send me to North Korea?" Theo asked sarcastically, shaking his head in disgust.

"Theo, it's like camp, not communism," his mother retorted.

"How can you even entertain this notion? They don't allow cell phones! Have you no mercy, woman?"

"Theo, stop the theatrics," Mr. Bartholomew interrupted as Theo dropped to his knees.

"Take a good look at this face; it may be the last time you *ever* see it."

"Theo, they are going to help you enjoy life more,

worry less. Doesn't that sound good?" his father asked calmly.

"Worry? Me? I don't worry. I am merely a practical observer of life, commenting on potential harms. That hardly constitutes worrying," Theo said in a vain attempt to convince his parents that he didn't have a problem.

"Theo," his parents said pityingly in unison.

"What?"

"You don't take the subway," his mother started.

"A fire could break out or someone could push me in front of a train; the mayor keeps ignoring my letters about a safety rail. And not to mention all the people touching stuff with their dirty hands. A lot of them don't use soap in the bathroom — you know the type: Joaquin. He runs his fingers under water for three seconds and thinks his hands are clean."

"What about wearing a parachute on planes?" his father asked.

"Preventative measure in case of engine trouble. I truly believe that it's the wave of the future."

"The surgical mask?" Mrs. Bartholomew asked sweetly.

"I only wear that during flu season. As any reputable

doctor will tell you, kids are more susceptible than adults. There were ninety-three influenza-related deaths in 2003."

"Is that what you're afraid of? Dying?"

"Until someone comes back and tells me what happens, I'm not sure I want to do it. And so far Grandma hasn't visited."

"Theo, why don't I explain a few things," his father said before expounding on the countless beliefs in the afterlife.

Theo sat calmly listening to everything his father had to say. Occasionally he nodded, or tilted his head, but mostly he just absorbed. Finally, when his father finished, Theo rubbed his chin and stared up at his parents.

"Do you feel better?" Mrs. Bartholomew asked hopefully.

"Not really. Don't you find it suspicious that the afterlife has more options than a salad bar?"

CHAPTER 3

EVERYONE'S AFRAID OF SOMETHING:

Illyngophobia is the fear of

vertigo or feeling dizzy when looking down.

Approximately one hundred seventy-nine miles from Manhattan was Roger Williams Elementary School in Providence, Rhode Island. Nestled on a quiet tree-lined street, miles from prestigious Brown University, was the traditional red schoolhouse that Lucy "Lulu" Punchalower attended. The twelve-year-old with strawberry blond hair, a healthy helping of freckles, and jade eyes had a penchant for speaking her mind, rolling her eyes, and generally antagonizing those around her.

When asked to describe Lulu, many of her classmates relied on a simple but effective term: "mean." While that was a fair assessment, it should be noted that Lulu was an inherently good person, though her overt acts of defiance masked that fact well. She was simply a bit of a rebel, right down to the bunched handcuffs she wore on her left wrist. The true purpose of the bracelets became known through a particularly eventful field trip to the Air and Space Museum.

Students have long held field trips in high regard, as they are days without lessons, classrooms, and homework. For this particular field trip, the sixth grade had voted to visit Providence's Air and Space Museum over the rather pedestrian Museum of Arts and Crafts. While the Museum of Arts and Crafts had a great deal more to it than dried macaroni ornaments, collages, and papier-mâché figures, the children thought the whole thing sounded a bit too much like an afternoon with their grandparents.

Before committing to the Air and Space field trip, Lulu conducted an investigation regarding the museum's elevator/stair situation. She perused the museum's Web site and called the information desk multiple times until she felt confident regarding her ability to access the stairs.

Of the twenty-four sixth graders arriving at the Air and Space Museum, all but Lulu were gulping down a sugary beverage. She refrained from food and drinks while out of the house to avoid having to use the restroom. Lulu found that most public restrooms occupied less square footage than a coffin and lacked windows. Therefore, she preferred to skirt the issue altogether. Slightly dehydrated, Lulu hung near the back of the herd of children as they slowed to a stop in the lobby of the museum.

Mr. Brampton and Mrs. Johnson were the teachers-slash-wranglers on this particular outing, and by the looks on their faces, they were not enjoying it.

"Quiet down, quiet down. I want everyone using inside voices," Mr. Brampton said. "Mrs. Johnson and I will be breaking the group in two for the elevator. And those of you with cell phones, consider yourselves warned: if I see or hear one, it will be confiscated, no exceptions."

From the back of the group came the distinctive jingle of Lulu's handcuffs as her arm shot straight in the air.

"Um, Mr. Brampton, I'd rather take the stairs; it's healthier."

"Unfortunately, the stairs are closed today, they're repainting."

"What? No one told me that. I would like to take the stairs anyway; paint fumes never hurt anyone," Lulu said as she felt a twitch behind her left eye, her regular reaction to stress. It wasn't that noticeable, but to Lulu it felt as if a boulder were pulsating beneath the thin flap covering her eye.

"That's not possible. You need to stay with the group, and we are taking the elevator."

"I am NOT taking the elevator. I'd rather stay right here."

"You will take the elevator like everyone else. As much as I would love to leave you down here, someone could kidnap you, and that wouldn't reflect well on the school."

"How will it reflect on the school when the parents find out you forced me into a steel death trap?"

"This is not a discussion, Ms. Punchalower, this is an order. Get in the elevator. And we will deal with your attitude when we get back to school."

"I will never, ever, ever, ever get in that or any other elevator, and you can't make me. I have a condition called claustrophobia. I can get you a doctor's note."

"I am not going to tell you again — get in the elevator."

"This is so unfair; you don't make Howie run in P.E."

"He has a broken leg!"

"Exactly, he has a condition that prevents him from running. I have a condition that prevents me from going in elevators and other confined spaces. Why is that so hard for you to understand?"

Mr. Brampton stared at Lulu and shook his head.

"Whatever, you can't *make* me do anything."

Mr. Brampton, now boiling with frustration, walked through the children, parting them like the Red Sea. When he finally reached Lulu, his six-foot-one frame dwarfed her body. Lulu's small crossed arms and twitching eye were imperceptible in the shadow of such a tall man. Mr. Brampton pushed her toward the open elevator without paying any mind to her incessant pleading.

Lulu's heart pounded ferociously. All she could feel was the suffocation of her breath and the cold metal of the cuffs against her skin. She dug her Converse sneakers into the floor futilely, trying to stop the wave bearing down upon her. The plastic soles squeaked loudly as she skidded across the concrete.

Lulu knew what she had to do. She had rehearsed this moment many times in her mind, a scenario she knew would eventually come. Perhaps not at this precise location or with these particular people, but she had always known it was coming. It was only a matter of time before someone would try to force her into an elevator, a bathroom without windows, or some other confined space.

Lulu's small body overflowed with adrenaline as she stealthily crouched down, falling between Mr. Brampton's legs. With the agility of an Olympic gymnast, she performed a backward somersault, bounced to her feet, and took off in a sprint. If any judges had been present, she could have easily scored a ten. Her small legs worked overtime to beat Mr. Brampton. Luckily, the man's bulky thighs rubbed together, slowing him down.

Lulu ducked beneath the body of a WWII bomber plane on the left side of the lobby. Mr. Brampton, consumed with catching Lulu, did not notice the plane until his forehead smashed into the body, leaving nail indentations above both of his eyebrows. His robust frame wavered back and forth before crashing to the cement floor. Lulu's classmates watched with rapt attention, absolutely thrilled by the excitement.

As her classmates reveled in the action, Lulu slapped the cuffs around the metal rod directly above the plane's wheels. Without any regard for her fallen teacher, Lulu sat down to catch her breath. A few feet away, Mr. Brampton stirred, grunted, and touched his forehead.

"You'll have to drag the plane along if you want to get me in the elevator," Lulu said with an abundance of pride in her well-executed plan.

Mr. Brampton, awash with animosity, hobbled silently toward the elevator. He didn't dare say a word for fear of what he would shriek. Profanity would most definitely be involved.

The following day, the dean confiscated Lulu's handcuffs and explained that she was banned from field trips for the remainder of her time at Roger Williams Elementary. The Punchalowers received a registered letter explaining that Lulu would have to stay home and write essays on the history of the elevator for the remaining two field trips.

The Punchalowers didn't mind their daughter's staying home or performing extra class work, but they loathed the idea of her classmates gossiping to their parents about Lulu's performance at the museum. The Punchalowers belonged to a set of parents whose favorite pastime was bragging about their children's accomplishments, and

Lulu's behavior hardly ranked as an achievement. Why, only a week after the infamous museum escapade, the Punchalowers were sure they heard whispering as they took to the golf course at the country club. Mrs. Punchalower had worked tirelessly to uphold the family's regal front, and now Lulu was jeopardizing it all.

After the museum episode, Lulu noticed an increased amount of murmuring in her overly tense home. She suspected her parents were up to something, but in all honesty, she didn't pay them much mind. It wasn't until the early weeks of May that Lulu found she could no longer disregard the suspicious activities of her routine-oriented parents. Not once in Lulu's twelve years of life had her parents fetched the mail. Lulu wasn't even sure how the mail got in the house; all she knew was that her parents never dared worry themselves with such trivial matters until now. Her parents suddenly *insisted* on being the first ones at the mailbox; under no circumstances were Lulu or her eight-year-old brother, Marvin, to approach the mailbox.

"Mom."

"What did I tell you about calling me that?" Mrs. Punchalower firmly rebuked her daughter.

"Fine, Mother," Lulu said with attitude, "let me get the mail."

"Absolutely not, young lady. You and your brother are prohibited from leaving the house until either your father or I have checked the mailbox. If I see either of you near the front door I will ground you for a month."

"Whatever."

"Whatever is not an appropriate response in any situation, and certainly not to your mother's instructions," Mrs. Punchalower rigidly responded.

"Yes, Mother dearest," Lulu said while rolling her green eyes back into her head.

Lulu's suspicions regarding the mail exploded on a nondescript Tuesday morning in early May, when she watched her parents dance with elation on the lawn. This was highly suspect behavior for a couple who thought dancing at weddings was in poor taste. Lulu knew it would have taken something monumental to provoke such peculiar behavior, and she was determined to get to the bottom of it.

Lulu ran to the end of hallway, lowered herself atop the immaculate cream-colored carpet, and waited. Her small head protruded from behind the wall, giving her a view of the formal living room. She heard the front door open swiftly, followed by the clacking of heels across the marble foyer. Lulu watched her parents whisper conspiratorially into each other's ears as they pushed a pink envelope back and forth between them. Mrs. Punchalower, rife with frustration, finally took the envelope and slipped it under the tartan couch cushion.

Moments later in the kitchen, Lulu spooned Raisin Bran into her mouth while watching her mother suspiciously. Lulu was certain that that pink letter had something to do with her. As Marvin followed her toward the bus stop, a nagging little voice dominated Lulu's thoughts. Instead of standing beneath the simple yellow sign with a black stencil of a bus as usual, Lulu dragged Marvin behind a row of nearby garbage cans.

"What are you doing?" Marvin complained as she pushed him to the ground.

"You're staying with me."

"No, I'm going to school. I have a math test."

"I know you; you'll tell Dotty I'm skipping if I let you go."

Marvin had a knack for telling people what they weren't supposed to know. If left alone on the bus he would positively tell Dotty, the bus driver, of Lulu's truancy.

"How long are we going to wait here?" Marvin whined.

"Until Mother and Father leave. I'm sure they're up to something."

"Who cares? We don't even like them. Let's go to school."

"Fine, but don't blame me if they sell you to Grandma."

"Sell *me*?" Marvin responded with shock.

"Grandma's been eyeing you for a while. She misses having a kid in the house. Plus, she needs someone to massage the bunions on her feet."

"How come Grandma doesn't want to buy you? You're older."

"What can I tell you? I'm not that cute anymore."

"I knew this face was going to get me into trouble," Marvin mumbled.

After watching their parents' cars pass, Lulu and Marvin crawled out from behind the trash cans and ran toward their house. Lulu fumbled with the keys, hoping that neither parent had forgotten anything. Finally, she opened the door and ran for the couch with Marvin close behind. Under the middle tartan cushion was the oblong pale pink envelope crafted out of expensive cardstock with formal gold printing on it.

The Punchalowers were part of the country club set and often received fancy invitations, but never in a color as vulgar as pink. Moreover, they never had hidden any of the invitations in the past. Lulu noticed the return address was a post office box in Farmington, Massachusetts. She didn't think her parents even knew anyone in Massachusetts, let alone someone with a post office box. Weren't those reserved for contest entry forms and wacky wilderness people miles from civilization?

Lulu slowly opened the envelope, pulling out an acceptance letter, brochure, and map. She wondered if her parents had finally decided to send her to boarding school as they often threatened. Her eyes narrowed and then bulged as she read the institution's name: School of Fear. She was to report to the Farmington, Massachusetts, bus station at 9:00 AM on Monday, May twenty-fifth, to meet a delegate from School of Fear.

With a hand over her twitching left eye, Lulu turned to Marvin. "I'm in big trouble; nothing good ever begins at a bus station."

School of Fear had come to Mrs. Punchalower's attention through a renowned specialist, Dr. Guinness. The doctor was a formidable man in his late fifties who sympathized immensely with Lulu's fears, but was unable to reason with her to enter his office on the fourth floor of an elevator-only building. Lulu tried to bully the security guard into letting her climb the fire escape, but he politely declined.

"If you don't let me on the fire escape, I swear, you'll never see your kids again," Lulu said in her best gangster impression.

"I don't have kids," the security guard said with a yawn.

"Um, I meant your wife."

"I don't have a wife."

"What about friends?"

"Don't have those either."

"Come on," Lulu said with frustration, "everyone has friends."

"Not me. All I have is a goldfish."

"Okay, loser," Lulu said with a roll of her eyes, "if you ever want to see that fish again, I suggest you let me on the fire escape. Otherwise, I'll be sautéing the little guy for dinner."

"Threatening a man's fish, that's cold, but you still can't go on the fire escape."

"Ugh!" Lulu huffed as she stormed out of the building; it was impossible to coerce a man whose only friend was a fish.

In a rather unorthodox move, Dr. Guinness agreed to conduct the sessions in his car in the parking lot. Instead of sitting on the therapist's couch, Lulu sat in the backseat and Dr. Guinness in the front. Occasionally, it grew so stuffy in the car, he turned on his noisy diesel-guzzling 1973 Mercedes to run the air-conditioning. Due to the strict doctor-patient confidentiality agreement, the windows could not be lowered more than a crack, lest someone walk by and eavesdrop.

After five months, Dr. Guinness had developed heat

rash, as well as a severe neck cramp from craning to see Lulu in the backseat. He requested a meeting with her parents in the car after Lulu's session.

"I'm afraid it's time to terminate my relationship with Lulu," Dr. Guinness calmly explained.

"What? You can't be serious. It's only been five months; my wife's been in therapy for ten years, and her doctor hasn't dumped her!" Mr. Punchalower fumed while simultaneously typing on his BlackBerry.

"Edward, please refrain from using the word *dump!*" Mrs. Punchalower retorted, "And Jeffrey is a *life coach*, not a therapist."

"I think you've misunderstood me. I believe that Lulu needs a more intense program than I can offer. Something very unique, very *exclusive*."

"Yes?" Mr. and Mrs. Punchalower said.

Their eyes lit up at the word "exclusive." Nothing pleased them more than being "exclusive."

"I'm talking about School of Fear," Dr. Guinness said in the quietest of all whispers.

CHAPTER 4

EVERYONE'S AFRAID OF SOMETHING:

Agyrophobia is the fear of

crossing the street.

Hidden deep within a rural pocket in Northwestern Massachusetts was a small town known as Farmington. For a lucky four hundred and four people, twenty-eight dogs, forty-nine cats, and six horses it was home. While there were many other creatures from squirrels to turtles living in the town, they weren't registered with the county and, therefore, didn't make the yearly census.

Farmington was oddly untouched by time. Missing were any signs of corporate America such as Wal-Mart,

Starbucks, or McDonald's. Instead, each shop was privately owned with hand-painted signs to prove it. There was one main street, rather straightforwardly called Main Street, on which sat McMillan's Grocery Store, the post office, Henry's newsstand, Farmy's diner, and the sheriff's office.

Nearly all of the four hundred and four human residents (and many of the animal ones) lived on the roads surrounding Main Street, creating an extremely tight-knit community. A few people inhabited the surrounding wilderness, only sporadically venturing into town for mail and provisions. The ever-elusive headmistress of the School of Fear, Mrs. Wellington, and her caretaker, Schmidty, lived the farthest from town, atop a four-acre plateau with two-hundred-foot protective granite cliffs on all sides. Scientists supposed the unusual granite mountain was the result of a glacier from the Cretaceous Period, which was approximately a really, really long time ago.

Mrs. Wellington's estate, Summerstone, acted as a beacon in the Lost Forest. Upon hearing the name Lost Forest, one might wonder how a forest could get lost. It doesn't walk, run, or skip, and one would assume it's too large for a park ranger to miss. In this case, *lost* does not refer to the forest itself, but rather to anyone or anything that enters it.

The townsfolk in Farmington referred to the Lost Forest as their very own Bermuda Triangle. At the request of park rangers, it was long closed with many NO TRESPASSING signs posted around the perimeter. The only two things that dared cross the forest were the Moon River and a scarcely used cobblestone road, which led straight to the base of Summerstone's Mountain.

Harold Wellington built Summerstone in 1952 as an isolated retreat for his wife, Edith. The eight-bedroom manor surrounded by persimmon, fig, orange, and cherry trees was located squarely in the center of the grounds. Mr. Wellington had spared no expense in the construction of Summerstone or its lavish decoration.

Rumors abounded of golden latrines and platinum light switches resting beside Renoirs or Monets, but none of it was true. Mrs. Wellington was far too eclectic and peculiar to indulge in such noticeably grand items. She much preferred to commission one-of-kind pieces such as tortoiseshell tables and portraits of her pets. Regardless of Mrs. Wellington's offbeat taste, Summerstone was the grandest structure Farmington had ever seen. Unfortunately, the locals were only able to admire the architecturally mesmerizing building from a distance, as Mrs. Wellington did not take kindly to visitors.

CHAPTER 5

EVERYONE'S AFRAID OF SOMETHING:

Ablutophobia is the fear of

washing or bathing.

John F. Kennedy Airport in New York City was in for quite a surprise the night the Mastersons arrived from London. Weary travelers wheeling suitcases, holding children's hands, and generally trying to make it through the maze of gates stopped in their tracks. They paused mid-sentence, mid-gait, mid-look, mid-breath to stare at Madeleine Masterson, her parents, and a plume of repellent.

Quite literally, a cloud of bug repellent lingered over Madeleine's veil-covered head, causing strangers to cough vociferously. Madeleine plowed through the highly congested terminal without batting an eyelash. Madeleine had long ago made peace with the price of spider protection.

The Masterson clan rushed through the terminal to catch their flight to Pittsfield, or as Farmingtonians called it, "the Pitts." While the Mastersons expected the plane to be little, they certainly never thought it would be *that little*. The plane was approximately the size and color of a New York City cab, only much more run-down. If the Mastersons hadn't been told otherwise, they would have thought the plane was en route to a demolition yard. Its wings were lopsided, leaning strongly to the left, and the windows were secured with silver duct tape.

Mr. Masterson felt a definite somersault in his stomach while looking over the plane. He wondered how any reasonable person could NOT be afraid of the aircraft, yet Madeleine wasn't. She wouldn't have minded if the plane had been called *Certain Death*. For Madeleine, the comprehensive fumigation of the plane's interior was far more important to worry about than a little thing like safety — although, it should be noted that

Mrs. Masterson only allowed Madeleine access to non-flammable repellent.

The entire Masterson clan remained silent throughout the fifty-seven-minute flight. Madeleine was much too frantic worrying that School of Fear would confiscate her repellents and netted veil to be bothered with idle chitchat. The veil and repellents had been with her so long they had become extensions of her own limbs. In fact, Madeleine would sooner consider a life without arms than one without bug repellent, although she would have to come up with a clever contraption to spray the repellent without arms.

Madeleine considered the many gruesome things she would endure for her repellent and veil, completely ignoring the plane's wild altitude fluctuations. Mr. and Mrs. Masterson's stomachs climbed into their throats, but Madeleine barely noticed. She was absorbed in a bargaining of sorts: Was the veil worth a toe? Five toes? A foot? A hand? A fingernail? A finger?

The plane continued to weather heavy turbulence until finally landing — although it felt more like crashing — in the Pitts. Mr. Masterson wobbled with queasiness as he deplaned directly onto the bumpy Tarmac.

"Maddie, are you sure you're not afraid of flying? I'm not terribly fond of it myself, especially after that ride. I am more than happy to travel by car, bus, train, or boat. It seems a great deal easier than attempting to exterminate the planet of bugs and spiders. Do you think you might be up for switching fears?" Mr. Masterson asked as his face started to regain color.

"Mummy, please tell Father to stop talking," Madeleine said in a small but authoritative voice.

"Arthur, please. No one is in the mood for your sense of humor. Or rather lack thereof."

As part of the Mastersons' standard travel practice, the family checked into a pre-exterminated bed-and-breakfast, which was in this case the Pretty Pitts Inn. The Mastersons had long since implemented a fumigation mandate for all travel accommodations. It required a great deal of preparation and considerable expense, but it was necessary for Madeleine to maintain any semblance of sanity.

In the pale green bathroom at the Pretty Pitts Inn, Madeleine brushed her teeth vigorously while scanning the walls for spiderwebs. On the other side of the wall, the still nauseated Mastersons inspected the sheets and pillowcase before assembling the mesh canopy. Madeleine entered the room in her pink dressing gown with a built-in veil, pumped off a few sprays of repellent, climbed into bed, and silently prayed for a bug- and spider-free night.

At 7:30 AM the following morning, the fatigued Masterson family boarded a bus for Farmington. The silver-sided bus was completely empty except for a handsome young boy named Garrison Feldman. At thirteen, he was big for his age, making him an ace in all things athletic, from soccer to baseball to football. He was somewhat of a local celebrity at his Miami middle school, and not just for his exploits on the field. His blond hair, tanned complexion, and blue eyes inspired more than a few girls to drop sappy love notes in his locker. The combination of his athletic prowess and extreme good looks made Garrison the most popular boy at Palmetto Middle School.

However, in between successes on the field and blushing girls in the hall, Garrison had developed quite the reputation for moodiness, often snapping at classmates for inconsequential things. One day following an impressive soccer match, two of Garrison's classmates,

Phil and Rick, approached with boogie boards hanging from their backs.

"Dude, you were awesome out there," Rick exploded with excitement usually reserved for NFL players. "You led us to victory again!"

Garrison offered a knowing nod; he was praised regularly for his leadership on the field.

"We brought our boogie boards; let's sneak down to the beach and hit the waves," Phil suggested.

"Nah, I'm not into it," Garrison responded coldly.

"Come on," Rick chimed in, desperate to pique Garrison's interest. "You never come."

"Yeah, the waves are really breaking today," Phil said with pleasure. "There's a warning up and everything."

A small but powerful ocean breeze blew across Garrison's face, weakening his knees as he stared into the boys' eyes. Small spots of light flitted across his vision as he struggled to remain standing.

"I heard the waves are nearly twenty feet high," Rick added.

Garrison's eyes fluttered into a cross-eyed expression as he fought to stand upright.

"Man, what's wrong with your face?" Rick asked with concern.

"Oh that? That was my impersonation of your mom," Garrison shot back defensively.

"That's harsh, man," Rick said seriously.

Garrison marched off the field, turning behind the gardener's shed, where he collapsed in a heap of sweat and guilt. As he sat on the grass with clammy hands, he prayed that Phil and Rick couldn't see him. He needed a second to compose himself, to banish all thoughts of the beach and its giant waves. Outside of his parents, no one knew that Garrison was petrified of water. Not drinking water or showering water, but any large body of water such as a lake, pool, or ocean. Embarrassingly, Garrison even broke out in a cold sweat watching re-runs of *Baywatch*.

The fear of water, hydrophobia, didn't fit with Garrison's tough image, and he knew it. All the players he had defeated in baseball, basketball, and soccer would taunt him mercilessly if they found out. He was certain his game would suffer greatly from the release of this information.

Garrison knew that time was running out; he needed to address his hydrophobia or risk discovery. So at four-thirty in the morning, he had crept from his room to the den, where his dad kept their only computer, a bulky old desktop. Much to his parents' chagrin, Garrison had forced his family to move to this beaten-down house due to its distance from the shore. Dressed in old sweats, Garrison searched the Internet for an efficient solution. His fingertips grazed the keys lightly to avoid waking his gruff parents.

Garrison's stomach gurgled stridently as he imagined confronting his fear and gaining his father's approval. Whichever program he chose, it needed to work. If it didn't, his father would use the failure as fodder for more put-downs. Garrison prodded through Web sites, struggling with conflicting emotions. The phobic part of him yearned to avoid water, yet his rational mind wanted nothing more than to tackle it and move on. After all, a boy in Miami could avoid the beach for only so long before people got suspicious.

Nearing dawn, Garrison's eyelids drooped heavily as he vigorously attempted to resist sleep. Frustrated and exhausted, he scanned a blog entitled "Who's Afraid of

Virginia Woolf or Anything Else?" He inspected three testimonials before stopping on one written by an eleven-year-old boy who overcame his sun phobia during a summer at School of Fear. So thorough was this boy's treatment that he was now a junior lifeguard at the beach.

Garrison's fatigue instantly disappeared as he searched the testimonial for a contact number. But in a flash, it was gone. The message literally evaporated before his drowsy eyes. For a second he wondered if he had dreamed the whole thing. Did he make up the boy who lived at night due to his sun aversion? Garrison rubbed his eyes and once again looked at the screen. A stern statement from the law offices of Munchauser and Son appeared, claiming the previous testimonial was a work of fiction.

A rock formed in Garrison's stomach, a hardened mound of shriveled-up hope. The rock grew larger by the second, pushing his internal organs against his skin. He looked at his stomach, half-expecting to see an outline of his spleen. Garrison paused and took a deep breath, allowing for a trickle of common sense to enter his head. Why would a law office bother to post a letter about a boy's overactive imagination?

Sensing there was more to the story, Garrison scoured the Web for any other mention of School of Fear, but found nothing. The lack of information only bolstered Garrison's belief that he had stumbled onto something. In his gut, he knew he had to find School of Fear, by any means necessary. By now, the sun had risen and Garrison could hear the buzzing of his parents' alarm clock. His father lumbered into the kitchen for coffee, immediately spotting a sleep-deprived Garrison at the computer in the adjoining den.

"You better not be buying junk on eBay," Mike Feldman warned as he poured instant coffee crystals into a mug.

In a moment of truly poor judgment, Garrison had swiped his dad's credit card to pay for a replica Joe DiMaggio baseball card. It wasn't that he didn't have the money; he simply couldn't use cash on the Internet. Not wanting to steal, he dropped a twenty in his dad's wallet and called it even. Not surprisingly, his father had an entirely different perspective on the transaction.

Garrison shifted on the plaid chair as he wondered how much he was willing to bet School of Fear could help him. Was his belief in School of Fear worth what he was about to put himself through? Before he could decide, he spit out the words that cemented his decision. "I need your help."

Having brought both of his parents into the fold about School of Fear, Garrison knew there was no turning back. His father had no respect for quitters, whether it was in sports, scrabble, or finding the elusive School of Fear. Together the three of them canvassed over half the child therapists listed in Miami's phonebook, questioning each and every one of them about School of Fear.

Some hung up without saying a word, while others flatly denied having heard of such a thing. The manner in which some blustered and stammered led the Feldmans to believe that Garrison's instincts were right. It was Garrison who happened to call Dr. Ernestina Franklin on that fateful Wednesday morning. After asking about School of Fear, Garrison waited to hear either a dial tone or the usual denial, but instead he heard something entirely different.

"Yes."

"You've heard of School of Fear?" he repeated in a state of shock.

Within twenty minutes, the Feldman family was pulling up to Dr. Franklin's quaint yellow home. Upon seeing the frail old woman at the door, they knew she was nearing both senility and death. Dr. Franklin greeted Garrison warmly with a hug and a kiss on the cheek. The old woman's overly welcoming manner was explained seconds later when she asked "Freddy" why he hadn't visited his grandma sooner.

Garrison, desperate for help, smiled and hugged his newfound grandma. He then covertly directed the conversation to the infamous School of Fear. Dr. Franklin's demeanor altered as she vaguely explained the mysterious institution. Garrison absorbed the information and attempted to ask questions, but Dr. Franklin refused to answer any of them. She did, however, agree to write "Freddy" — who Mrs. Feldman explained preferred to go by his middle name, Garrison — a letter of recommendation.

Letter in hand, the family was walking toward the front door when Dr. Franklin stopped them.

"Wait!" the old woman shouted as she opened the end table's drawer.

She held up a small and withered photograph. The

Feldmans approached slowly, unsure what to expect. First Mr. Feldman, then Mrs. Feldman, and finally Garrison gasped at the sight of a man's distorted face. Knobs of scaly flesh covered his cruel face. Almost worse than his skin were his eyes; they weren't the typical bloodcurdling black, but a much more disconcerting banana yellow.

"Once you send that letter, he'll be watching you . . . everywhere you go, everything you buy, anyone you call, he'll know; he knows everything," Dr. Franklin said ominously.

"Who?" Garrison asked quietly.

"Munchauser."

CHAPTER 6

EVERYONE'S AFRAID OF SOMETHING:

Hippopotomonstrosesquippedaliophobia

is the fear of long words.

In a feeble attempt to impress his insult-prone father, Garrison had insisted on riding the bus alone. While Mrs. Feldman thought it was too dangerous for a thirteen-year-old boy to travel alone, Mr. Feldman pointedly said that the boy needed to adhere to the strict guidelines of both the NBA and NFL: "No Babies Allowed" and "No Freaking Losers." These two tidbits, according to Mr. Feldman, were words of wisdom to live your life by, and he shared them with Garrison at least three times a day. He saw it as his parental duty to toughen the boy up, because success never came to babies or losers, on the field or in life.

Garrison savored the notion of a sports-acronym, insult-free summer while quietly reading his *Baseball Today* magazine on the bus. Mr. Masterson, a few rows behind Garrison, couldn't help but watch the boy as he read. Next to him, Mrs. Masterson fought the desire to sleep, desperately trying to keep her eyes from closing. Every few seconds her eyelids would descend slowly, covering half her eyes, before the sharply dressed woman would snap back awake. As Mrs. Masterson roused back to consciousness, Mr. Masterson leaned in to whisper in his wife's ear.

"Do you think that boy is heading to *the place*?"

"I can't imagine any other reason for being on a bus in the Pitts at this ungodly hour," Mrs. Masterson responded.

"He looks so normal," Mr. Masterson continued while inspecting the blond boy's exterior.

"Darling, fears don't always manifest themselves in such overt manners like our Maddie," Mrs. Masterson said as her eyelids once again descended.

"Quite right," Mr. Masterson said, peering over at his veiled daughter.

Garrison, oblivious to the conversation behind him, continued reading and eating the tuna sandwich his mother had made for him. As he absorbed players' batting averages, he heard the rattle of the bus crossing a metal grate. Instinctively, Garrison looked out his window. From the view, he could tell the bus was on a bridge. His palms sweated profusely while his tuna-filled stomach churned and cramped. Bridges usually span breadths of water, but not always.

Garrison prayed for a dry ravine or, better yet, that he could resist looking altogether. His anxiety increased rapidly, moving him closer to the window, directing his eyes downward. Garrison saw blue. And lots of it. There was, of course, a window and at least one hundred feet protecting Garrison from the water, but it didn't matter. The unraveling of reason was instantaneous.

"No," Garrison mumbled aloud.

Sweat patches formed on his face, dripping off his eyebrows, clouding his already blurred vision. Spots of light further obstructed his sight as panic arrested his lungs. Garrison's wheezing caught the Mastersons' attention, but before they could ask if he was all right, he screamed. His voice hit a decibel rarely heard outside of rock concerts.

"Wwwwwwaaaaaaattttteeeerrrr!"

The surreal sensation of drowning took hold, forcing Garrison to gasp for air while flailing his arms. He was sure his face was a crimson mess. However, before he could check, it went black. The young boy fainted facedown in the aisle, and not a very clean aisle at that. His beautiful tanned face landed right between a putrid-looking green stain and an old piece of chewing gum.

Mr. Masterson ran to Garrison, checked his pulse, and dabbed his damp and dust-covered forehead. He promptly lifted Garrison onto a seat, placing his head across Mrs. Masterson's lap. She gently brushed his moist hair off his face as Madeleine stared dreamily at the boy.

"Mummy, can we keep him?" Madeleine asked with the wide eyes of a burgeoning crush.

"Darling, little boys make terrible pets," Mrs. Masterson offered with a wink.

"That's not true at all, Mummy. They're hypoallergenic, much easier than dogs," Madeleine said cheekily, "and they almost never have fleas."

Madeleine stepped closer to Garrison, pressing her veiled face against his flushed cheek. Starstruck and utterly enamored, she could have spent hours digesting the boy's features, but the soft tickle of her netting stirred Garrison back to consciousness. As Garrison cracked his groggy eyes open, uncertainty and confusion quickly flashed across his face. He wasn't sure what had happened, but there was a peculiar head pressed against his, and it was freaking him out.

"Ugh!" Garrison mumbled, and he jerked away from Madeleine.

Much as a police officer would his gun, Madeleine drew her repellent and prepared to shoot. Clearly, she had come to think of her spray as a viable means of protection against anything. Garrison stared curiously, unsure what to make of the girl with a veil and belt of repellents.

"I assume you're also en route to," Mrs. Masterson then whispered, "School of Fear."

"Yeah. As you can tell, I don't really like water," Garrison mumbled while returning Madeleine's intense gaze.

"I'm terrified of spiders, bugs, and all such creatures," Madeleine shyly chimed in, attempting to relate.

Madeleine continued to stare, making Garrison even more uncomfortable and self-conscious than he already was. After all, two minutes ago, he'd woken up with his head in a stranger's lap and a veiled face pressed against his own. All in all, it had been a rather uneasy series of events. Madeleine zealously maintained her gaze, prompting Garrison to divert his eyes. While taking in the empty bus, it occurred to him that he could simply return to his seat to escape the rampant awkwardness.

"Well, I better . . ." Garrison stumbled over his words as he started back to his seat.

"Do you have any other fears? Besides water?" Madeleine asked, desperate to keep the young man in conversation.

"Nope."

"Oh, shame," Madeleine said with disappointment before realizing she had said it aloud. "In London 'shame' means great," she poorly covered.

"Darling?" Mrs. Masterson said with a confused look. "What on Earth are you talking about?"

"Mummy," she said sternly, pleading with her eyes for her mother to go along with the ruse.

"It was a *shame* to meet you, young man," Mrs. Masterson said with a mischievous expression.

Madeleine turned to her mother, cheeks scarlet red, and giggled.

While Garrison may have been embarrassed, he was also overwhelmingly relieved that his father was not present for his freak-out. He imagined the chorus of advice on life: NBA and NFL. In short, life doesn't reward babies or losers, and considering what had just transpired, Garrison felt like both. He was so preoccupied by his feelings that he hardly noticed Madeleine watching him with the steady eye of an owl.

Madeleine was enraptured by Garrison's tan complexion, which greatly differed from the pale boys of London. It wasn't actually the boys' fault, as the whole of the United Kingdom was under a cloud for much of the year. But at that moment, Madeleine decided that boys, like bread, were better toasted.

Close behind Madeleine and Garrison on Route 7 were Theo and his mother. Mr. Bartholomew had requested to join them on the trip but was flatly denied by Theo.

"Dad, if you come and there's a car accident, you both could die and I could live. Then what? How would I go on? How would my brothers and sisters continue without the love and guidance of a parent? I mean really, Dad! How can you be so selfish?"

"Theo, nothing is going to happen to your mother or me. I promise."

"You promise? Dad, you are so naïve. Life is unpredictable. I'm sorry, but we simply cannot take this chance. You will remain at home."

"But, Theo," Mr. Bartholomew grumbled.

"No buts! My decision is final," Theo retorted.

"Okay, Theo. Whatever you say."

Once safely on the road, Theo scrutinized his mother, looking for any perceptible signs of fatigue. It was much harder than he expected, for riding in cars had always made him drowsy. As he stared at his mother's face, his eyelids weighed heavily, closing for seconds at a time.

His head bobbed back and forth as he blubbered, "What if you doze off and kill both of us?"

"Theo, I'm fine."

"Do you know how many people die in sleep-related accidents each year?"

Before Theo could tell his mother that according to the National Highway Traffic Safety Administration, drowsy driving was responsible for a minimum of 100,000 accidents each year, he drifted to sleep. This was just one of the oodles upon oodles of statistics Theo used to validate his many neuroses.

Only a couple miles behind Theo and his mother on Route 7 was the Punchalower family, who had hired a black town car to ferry them to Farmington. Mrs. Punchalower and Lulu tried to sleep but found it impossible with Mr. Punchalower's rapid typing on his BlackBerry. It was nothing short of a miracle that the man hadn't developed BBT (BlackBerry thumb), which causes the thumbs to freeze in a bent position. According to The Institute of BBT, if the BlackBerry trend continues, opposable thumbs could be obsolete within a century. Lulu held her throbbing left eye as she listened to her father type, all the while worrying that she would be forced to partake in "exercises" involving small, cramped spaces without windows.

"How do you know this camp isn't going to torture

me? Lock me in closets?" Lulu asked with an unsteady voice.

"Lucy Punchalower, I expect rational thinking from my children. Don't disappoint me," Mr. Punchalower said sternly without looking up from his BlackBerry.

"Do you guys know anyone who has gone to this strange school?" Lulu demanded.

"This institution comes highly recommended by Dr. Guinness. It's extremely *exclusive*," Mrs. Punchalower said with pride. "Your father and I expect you to do your best. Is that understood, young lady?"

"Whatever," Lulu huffed with frustration.

"What did I tell you about that word?" Mrs. Punchalower asked angrily.

"Are you saying that I am not allowed to say the words 'what' and 'ever' or just when they're together?" Lulu asked sarcastically.

"Any more lip and I will personally request they lock you in a closet," Mr. Punchalower said without an ounce of humor.

Lulu closed her eyes in an attempt to block out her parents. She tuned out her father's typing and focused on the sound of air pounding against the speeding car.

While Lulu didn't have any problem blocking out her parents, her fears were quite another story.

Questions stormed her mind, intensifying the thumping behind her eye. What if the bathroom didn't have a window? What if her bedroom was a converted closet? What if there was an elevator? Lulu longed to be back in her bedroom in Providence. When Lulu stayed home, she forgot entirely that she was claustrophobic.

The Punchalower family drove down Farmington's idyllic Main Street, a scene akin to a Norman Rockwell painting. The black town car stopped in front of the bus station at exactly 8:57 AM. As Lulu exited the car, she noticed a young boy hysterically crying and hugging his mother. It was a desperate, emotion-filled hug most often seen in dramatic love stories. Lulu was shocked by the display. As a byproduct of her rigid parents, Lulu never cried. In fact, she loathed crying altogether, prompting her to recoil as she passed the blubbering boy.

"Don't leave me here!" Theo screamed. "They could be criminals!"

Lulu paused at the word "criminal," realizing that the weeping boy had a point: she didn't have a clue what she was walking into.

CHAPTER 7

EVERYONE'S AFRAID OF SOMETHING:

Didaskaleinophobia is the fear of

going to school.

At 9:00 AM, Farmington's bus station was completely vacant except for Madeleine, Lulu, Theo, their respective parents, and Garrison. Seated alone on a pew, Garrison quietly read his baseball magazine in an attempt to ignore Madeleine's ogling. Mr. and Mrs. Masterson stood next to Madeleine, trying their best to breathe regularly as she sprayed copious amounts of repellent. The Punchalowers, seated in the pew across from Garrison, maintained severe expressions while

Lulu focused on Theo's quivering cheeks. Lulu found it indefensible to cry in public. She was a Punchalower and Punchalowers didn't cry. As a matter of fact, she wasn't even sure they had tear ducts.

The bus station's arched wooden door creaked open with the guttural growl of a feral cat. All four children turned, expectantly waiting to see the next School of Fear student arrive. Their eyes focused on the dark brown cowboy boots before moving up to khaki slacks and finally stopping on an obscenely large gun holster. Theo's heart beat fast, as it always did, in the presence of a deadly weapon. On the verge of screaming, he noticed a shiny badge on the man's chest; this was the sheriff. He was approximately forty-five years old with a long moustache that hung over his mouth. As if preparing for a speech, the sheriff cleared his throat to get everyone's attention.

"Hello, I'm Sheriff John McAllister, Farmington's law enforcement, dog trainer, and driver for the town's only car service. I will be escorting the four of you to School of Fear's campus a few miles out. As stated in the brochure, parents are not allowed to accompany students to the campus, so you are going to need to say your good-byes here."

"Hey Sheriff," Garrison said while raising his hand, "will we be driving over any water? Or next to it?"

"Son, I have been made aware of all of your situations and have taken precautions so that each of you will have an enjoyable journey."

"Would anyone object to a covering of bug repellent in the automobile?"

"I assume, miss, that you are Madeleine Masterson — fear of spiders, insects, and generally anything that crawls."

"That is most accurate, sir."

"As long as no one else objects, you are more than welcome to spray away. It's the white van out front."

"Are we waiting on other students?" Lulu asked hopefully.

"Today's trip is only the four of you. Remember, you must leave all electronic equipment such as cell phones, computers, BlackBerries, Sidekicks, pagers, Game Boys, et cetera with your parents."

Theo opened his mouth, then scrunched his face in a

silent howl while frantically clinging to his mother's leg. Life without a cell phone meant being completely removed from all that he held dear, and he simply couldn't stand for that. Theo was many things, but a passive observer of life was not one of them.

"Mom, *please* let me keep my cell phone. I will put it on silent and hide it from them. This man is suspicious, don't you think? He looks a lot like that guy we saw on the FBI's most wanted list at the post office. Actually, on second glance, it *is* him! I'd recognize those child-hating eyes anywhere. I'll distract him while you get the car. Go!"

"For Heaven's sake, Theo, he's the sheriff!"

"That's his cover — smart, isn't it? But not smart enough to fool us. Let's get out of here."

"You are not going anywhere."

"Don't you remember the poster? We are in the presence of a certified class-A maniac who tortures chubby kids with glasses."

"I don't remember the poster mentioning anything about chubby kids with glasses."

"We don't have time to debate this; we need to hit the road. Seriously, we should have left three seconds ago!"

"Your imagination is out of control."

"Some say imagination, others say psychic vision. Are you really willing to take that chance on your youngest, most sensitive son?"

"I'm pretty sure we ruled out all psychic abilities after the Yosemite trip. Now listen carefully, you aren't getting out of this, do you understand me?"

"Then show some mercy, woman! Let me keep my cell phone!"

Theo's plump face was fraught with desperation and anxiety. Mrs. Bartholomew wanted to appease his frantic mind, but she couldn't. The application to School of Fear was explicit about adhering to the rules and restrictions. It clearly stated that any child found in possession of contraband would face immediate expulsion without refund and possible legal action from the offices of Munchauser and Son. Moreover, if Theo were ever to lead a normal life, he needed to face his fears. Mrs. Bartholomew would never forgive herself if she impeded his treatment by allowing a cell phone.

"I'm sorry, Theo, but I can't let you take the cell phone."

Parked directly in front of the station was the

sheriff's large white van with massive black rubber bumpers along the sides and a rusted metal hook on its roof. It more closely resembled a bumper car than a normal passenger van. Madeleine and her father climbed into the vehicle and began the extermination. Mr. Masterson covered his face with his shirt and prayed that this was the last time he would ever have to exterminate anything again.

Standing outside the van, Lulu made claims on the window seat across from the sliding door. She often fretted about being trapped during a car accident and, therefore, preferred to sit near an exit. Garrison stared at Theo madly gripping his mother's leg, his face awash in tears. Sure, Garrison was afraid of water, but crying like a baby was something he, much as Lulu, couldn't understand. A horrific desire to extol Theo on the rules of life, NBA and NFL specifically, abounded as he watched the boy blubber.

"Don't worry, young man; the sheriff has assured me that there is no water on the way to the school. Apparently he is taking a route that avoids even the faintest view of the river," Mrs. Masterson said, unknowingly breaking Garrison's concentration on Theo.

Mr. Masterson and Madeleine had nearly finished with the van when they came across a rotund brown-and-white English bulldog on the floor of the driver's seat. Madeleine gasped, stirring the dog, who then stared at the young girl with saggy eyes and a pronounced under bite.

"Sheriff, it appears a dog has snuck into the car," Madeleine announced in her proper British accent.

"That's Mrs. Wellington's dog, Macaroni; he's here to check your bags."

"The dog's name is Macaroni?" Lulu scoffed.

"Yeah, Macaroni was part of a pair, but Cheese died last year."

"She had dogs named Macaroni and Cheese?" Garrison said. "Weird."

"Line up your bags. Macaroni will be sniffing for electronics," the sheriff announced.

Theo's small face twitched with alarm and apprehension as his mother placed his brown leather satchel next to the others. The bag had been a gift from his father for his tenth birthday, something Theo had wanted for ages. Yet today as Theo stared at the expensive satchel, he felt nothing but horror.

Then something occurred to Theo. Why had he never heard of an electronics-sniffing dog? Why weren't airports using them? Maybe this was all an elaborate ruse to trick the students into dumping their electronic ties to the outside world.

Macaroni waddled over to Madeleine's gray-and-black plaid bag and began sniffing leisurely, making his way from the top to the bottom. Macaroni employed an audible sniff, channeling all his energy into each inhalation. He toddled away from Madeleine's luggage, paused, and then returned to it. He performed one last long sniff before approaching Garrison's white nylon backpack with a Miami Heat logo. Macaroni inspected Garrison's bag at record speed; apparently, nylon is a much easier material to scrutinize. However, Macaroni did lick the bag with his wide purple tongue.

Understandably, Garrison frowned before proclaiming, "Gross."

Macaroni continued his rapid inspection pace with Lulu's green canvas sack. He managed to sniff his way from left to right and top to bottom in under a minute flat. And even better, he didn't feel the need to use his tongue. Now only Theo's academic leather satchel remained. Macaroni abandoned his fast pace, instead employing a thorough inhalation of each square inch of the bag. Five, then ten minutes passed as Macaroni sniffed and licked.

Theo felt his nerves ease, realizing that an electronics-smelling dog was patently absurd. He paused, thinking how awfully foolish and gullible of him it was to believe such a story. The portly old dog couldn't smell a bowl of batteries if it was under his nose. As Theo broke into a smile, Macaroni stopped to stare at the boy ominously. Theo's nerves cracked like an old piece of chewing gum as the sheriff unzipped the leather bag and Macaroni plunged headfirst. Seconds later, the dog emerged with a black sock in his drool-infested mouth.

"This dog *clearly* has no credibility. He's fishing out socks," Theo bellowed, walking toward the dog with his hand extended.

Mere inches from the sock, the sheriff's arm swooped in and grabbed the garment. He quickly reached into the sock and pulled out a sleek black cell phone. All eyes turned to Theo, who immediately threw his hands up in the air.

"I've been set up," Theo said spectacularly.

"Theo?" Mrs. Bartholomew asked incredulously.

"Mom, I don't know what kind of a scam these people are trying to pull, but we should leave," Theo said seriously.

"I am only going to ask you this once. Where did you get that phone?"

"This is a setup. The so-called sheriff and the dog are behind it. . . ." Theo trailed off before relenting under his mother's unsympathetic gaze. "It's unreasonable to spend an entire summer without a phone. People need phones. It's as natural as water or air!"

"I'm truly sorry, Sheriff. I don't know where he got that cell phone. I already confiscated his personal one," Mrs. Bartholomew explained, ignoring Theo entirely.

"The black market! That's where you forced me to go," Theo said angrily.

"You bought this on the street?"

"Well, not technically. But in spirit, yes."

"Theo?" Mrs. Bartholomew pressed on with mounting irritation.

"Fine. I got it off eBay, but it's still dangerous."

"For Heaven's sake, Theo," Mrs. Bartholomew said with embarrassment.

Without any further ado, Madeleine lifted her veil, kissed her parents on the cheek, and entered the van. She took the left seat in the back row, pulled down her veil, and sprayed a circle around her feet. Without anyone to say goodbye to, Garrison quickly followed Madeleine, taking the seat on the right.

Lulu turned to her parents, unsure how to say goodbye. Mr. Punchalower set the tone by releasing his left hand from his BlackBerry for a cordial handshake. Lulu rolled her eyes, shook his hand, and approached her rigid mother. Lulu believed that her mother secretly longed to hug her but couldn't in front of her father. Whether true or not, that's what Lulu told herself as she held her mother's cold and bony hand.

Once Lulu was seated, Theo hugged his mother, gulped down tears, and stepped into the van. His overt lack of drama surprised everyone, even Theo. Perhaps this journey would offer him a chance to mature. Just as soon as the thought crossed Theo's mind, he smashed his face against the window and howled. Clearly, maturity would have to wait.

CHAPTER 8

EVERYONE'S AFRAID OF SOMETHING:

Optophobia is the fear of

opening one's eyes.

Theo banged his fists against the window as the van pulled away. It was reminiscent of many a prison drama he had watched with his grandmother before her death. Panic seized Theo as he imagined never seeing his mother again. He buried his face in his hands, much to the annoyance of Lulu and Garrison, who exchanged telling looks. Madeleine didn't mind at all, although it was near impossible to read her expression through the veil and cloud of repellent.

"Hey, I totally get that you are afraid of spiders, but I am about to pass out from the fumes," Garrison said.

Madeleine blushed with mortification and nodded before turning toward the opposite window.

"Do you have a cell phone, Sheriff?" Theo asked with tears running down his cheeks.

"I do, but it's only for emergencies."

"This is an emergency. I need to make sure nothing has happened to my mom."

"Theo, nothing has happened to your mom. It's been five minutes. She hasn't even had enough time to pull out of the parking lot! So STOP crying," Lulu screamed.

"Yeah," Garrison added, "you're acting like such a baby. It's pathetic."

Theo concentrated, desperate to stop crying so Lulu and Garrison wouldn't attack him again, but somehow he couldn't. The more he tried, the harder it got. Theo closed his eyes and resolved to cry.

The weeks leading up to School of Fear had been filled with much dread and anticipation for Lulu, Madeleine,

Theo, and Garrison. So it was hardly a surprise that within minutes of leaving the station, the foursome fell sound asleep. Madeleine's veiled head bobbed forward, moving to the bumps in the road. A river of drool poured steadily from the left corner of Theo's mouth, down his chin, and onto his shirt. Garrison's face was pressed against the window, distorting the shape of his eyes and ears. As for Lulu, even in her sleep she managed an annoyed expression.

High-pitched squeals forced the snoozing students awake. One by one, they parted their eyelids, uncertain what to expect. Three pudgy squirrels decorated the windshield of the stationary van. Thankfully, the furry brown creatures weren't dead, merely a little dazed. The sheriff wasn't concerned; in fact, he turned and winked at the students.

"What the heck are those?" Theo screeched.

"Nothing to worry about, just some flying squirrels."

"Excuse me sir, with all due respect as I am not a zoologist, I assure you that squirrels cannot fly," Madeleine interjected.

"Well, that's true. I should probably call them gliding squirrels. They leap off trees and use a flap of skin between their feet and hands like a parachute, but as you can see, they don't have the best aim. At least five squirrels crash into my van every time I drive up here. Luckily, they're fat little guys; doesn't hurt them much."

"Kind of like Theo," Garrison mumbled under his breath.

Theo sneered at Garrison before noticing the world outside the car. Garrison, Lulu, and Madeleine followed Theo's stunned gaze. It was dark, as one would expect late in the evening, not the morning. Their young eyes searched for sky, even a small square, but there was none. Lulu felt a twitch behind her left eye as her breaths grew shorter and more labor-intensive.

"Are we underground?" Lulu asked as she grabbed her eye.

"Not at all, it's just the vines; they block all the light."

Leafy vines grew from one tree-lined side of the road to the other, creating a tunnel.

"Um, so when are we getting out of here?" Lulu asked tensely.

"Very soon," the sheriff reassuringly explained as he started the van up again.

Madeleine lifted her veil and squinted to see the cobblestone road on which the van traveled. As if the thick trees, excessive vines, and lack of light weren't creepy enough, there were loads of handmade signs warning against entering the forest.

"What kind of vine grows like this?" Garrison asked while pushing blond locks off his tan forehead.

"Sticky vines. They can trap a man with their sap. For a while they were mining it for superglue, but that didn't work out very well," the sheriff said vaguely.

"What happened?" Madeleine asked.

"Cost them too many men."

"They died?" Theo asked with fright.

"Worse. Their hair got stuck in the vines and the men had to shave their heads. And there were some ugly heads with craters and lumps and birthmarks. A couple of their wives left them. Word got out and soon no one would come near the place, so the factory went under."

"And this is where the School of Fear is located? Doesn't seem very child-friendly," Theo tweeted nervously.

"Don't worry, the school's not down here," the sheriff answered calmly.

The road suddenly dead-ended in a small spot of sunlight at the base of a sheer granite cliff. So smooth was the gray-specked rock that there was a hazy reflection of the car on its surface.

"It's on top of the mountain. The forest just surrounds it," the sheriff said calmly.

"What? How do we get up there? I'm not a certified rock climber," Theo said with a touch of hyperventilation. "I know we all eventually die, but I don't want to die climbing a mountain, especially without a cell phone."

"Theo, chill. I'm sure there's stairs or something," Lulu said hopefully. "Maybe an escalator? 'Cause I am not getting in an elevator, Sheriff. Understand?"

"We're here," the sheriff said into a CB radio on the dashboard before turning to Theo and Lulu. "You have my word; there will be no rock climbing or elevator."

An unfamiliar noise startled the students, rattling their already raw nerves. The sound of metal grinding above their heads prompted them to gape dumbfounded at the van's ceiling. The crunching of metal abruptly stopped, and the van lifted off the cobblestone road, jiggling the students' every bone and muscle.

"This can't be happening," Theo mumbled to himself before closing his eyes, desperate to block out the situation.

"Almost there, guys," the sheriff said reassuringly as the van was lowered onto the platcau.

The first thing they saw when they opened their eyes was approximately twenty-five feet high and constructed out of splintering wood. It was the crane that had pulled them up the mountain, and frankly, it didn't look strong enough to lift a bouquet of flowers. At the base of the crane, in a small operating booth, was an old man, a seriously old man. Maybe the oldest man in the state, or at least he looked that way from twenty feet away.

"There must be a better way to get up here than that," Lulu said.

"Seriously, Sheriff, build a road!" Garrison blurted out.

"If it ain't broke, why fix it," the sheriff responded.

"Save your silly sayings for someone else. That thing is death on a hook. I felt like a fish being reeled in! Just look at that thing. When was the last time it was inspected?" Theo asked seriously. "I am making a mental note to contact the building department. Do you hear me, Sheriff?"

The mountaintop was enclosed by a soaring stone wall, lined by eerily still crows gazing toward Farmington in the distance. Madeleine had the sensation of being on an island in the sky, far removed from anything she knew. Quietly she prayed that the high altitude and sheer cliffs kept spiders and insects at bay.

The van passed under the stonewall arch, bringing Summerstone, in all its glory, into view. Lulu, Madeleine, Theo, and Garrison could not explain why the intricate molds of the mansion's limestone façade or the patchy green grass intimidated them so greatly, but it did. Even the overgrown shrubs prompted the hairs on the back of their necks to stand up. While admittedly creepy and poorly maintained, the mansion retained a certain regality with its stunning architecture and vast size. A few coats of paint and a gardener would do wonders for the place.

The sheriff slowly drove up the gravel path, allowing the children to drink in their surroundings, before stopping in front of the mansion's formal entrance. A wooden door eight feet wide and twenty feet high with an owl cast-iron knocker added to the imposing tone. To the right and left of the door were large glass lanterns hanging from rusted gold chains.

The old man from the crane waddled up the stairs, stopping in front of the gargantuan door. While the man's long-expired driver's license listed him at five foot nine, a large boil at the base of his neck brought him down to five foot five. Polyester black slacks belted below his armpits made his chest less than six inches in length. Over the years, the man's belly had expanded, and in a vain attempt to hide it he hiked up his trousers. Even worse than the man's fashion sense was the long wisp of gray hair that wrapped around the top of his head like a turban. If unwound, the hair would surely hang below his shoulders. It was by far the most elaborate comb-over in New England.

"Well, here we are, kids," the sheriff announced from the front seat of the van.

"Who is that *weird*-looking guy?" Garrison questioned the sheriff.

"That's Schmidty, Summerstone's caretaker."

"This doesn't look anything like the brochure," Lulu said with irritation.

Madeleine and Theo remained silent, but their faces mirrored Lulu's shocked expression. Clearly all four of them had received the same brochure of beautiful, manicured grounds filled with children running and playing. This was an isolated, dark manor well past its prime.

A stunned Lulu exited the van first, followed quickly by an alarmed Theo. He wanted to cry, but he worried that Lulu would scold him again. She was a little scary. Garrison exited, grateful that there didn't appear to be a pool, and Madeleine remained in the car with her hands politely folded in her lap.

Noticing her lack of movement, the sheriff stuck his head back into the van.

"Sir, I would prefer to stay in the van. The outside looks particularly spider-friendly."

"I'm afraid that's not possible, young lady. I need to take the van back into town. But don't worry; Schmidty's going to take you inside now to meet your teacher."

Madeleine's stomach churned wildly as she climbed over the seat and prepared to exit the van. She had to depart or the anticipation would make her vomit. Madeleine placed her right, then her left foot on the cement steps. She sprayed repellent wildly as the old man opened the front door.

"Sheriff, before you depart, I'll need Mac back," Schmidty announced formally.

"Of course, almost forgot."

The fat dog ambled out of the front seat and into the fog Madeleine had created. Displeased by the air quality, Macaroni released a low-level growl to clear his throat.

"See you in six weeks, kids," the sheriff said before waving goodbye.

"Six weeks?" Garrison mumbled in response to the sheriff.

None of them could imagine lasting the hour, let alone six weeks at this place.

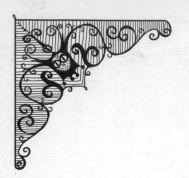

CHAPTER 9

EVERYONE'S AFRAID OF SOMETHING:

Cacophobia is the fear of

ugliness.

Summerstone's foyer was unusually spacious with pink fleur-de-lis wallpaper peeling from the ceiling. Aside from the drooping wallpaper, the room was pristinely maintained and incredibly clean. Much to Madeleine's relief, there wasn't a cobweb in sight. Still, as a precaution, she sprayed a circle around her feet, causing the others to inch away. Schmidty left the children in the foyer in order to lower the sheriff off the mountain with the crane.

The foursome stood awkwardly around an oval chestnut table with a vase of pink hydrangeas. As they surveyed the room, it was hard to ignore the far wall decorated with pictures of beauty queens with beehive hairdos, crowns, sashes, and extremely shiny teeth. Shoes clacking across a wooden floor interrupted the students' inspection of their new surroundings. At the top of the sweeping staircase, an elderly woman in a powder blue knee-length skirt and matching jacket stood femininely with her right leg slightly bent, as if posing for a photograph.

The woman's clothes, like the interior of the house, dated from the mid-to-late 1950s. With four sets of eyes on her, she delicately and pretentiously sashayed down the staircase. Theo, Madeleine, Garrison, and Lulu had no way of knowing what to expect, since so far nothing had been what they'd thought it was going to be.

As the woman approached, her sagging paper-thin skin came into focus. She had clearly invested an enormous amount of time applying makeup to hide her age. The woman had bubblegum pink lips, thick black eyeliner, fake eyelashes, and light blue eye shadow that matched her outfit. Madeleine, grateful she hadn't lifted her veil, stared freely at the peculiar-looking woman in a brown bob wig.

Lulu stifled laughter as she noticed tortoiseshell

glasses hanging from a gold chain around the woman's neck. Not even Lulu's grandmother in Boca Raton wore her glasses on a chain. Trailing behind the woman as she made her grand entrance were four cats — two black and two gray. She paused in front of the students and waited for the cats. Once all the felines were down the stairs, the old woman began.

"Hello, I am Mrs. Wellington, your teacher, headmistress, and all-around center of the universe at School of Fear," she said in a haughty tone. "I assume you have already met Schmidty, the groundskeeper slash cook slash office assistant. He's nearly blind, so if you make a snide face at him, he'll hardly notice. As for Mac, he's still recovering from the death of his partner, Cheese, so be kind. I should add that only Schmidty and I are to call him Mac; he's Macaroni to you. And the cats — Fiona, Errol, Annabelle, and Ratty — are my greatest achievement, literally living proof of my teaching abilities. I trained these cats. And if I can train a cat, I can definitely train you."

"What have you trained them to do?" Lulu asked.

"To behave completely untrained. Quite exemplary if I may say so myself," Mrs. Wellington said with a cackle.

"Are we being filmed? Is this a reality show? Our parents' idea of a joke?" Garrison asked sincerely.

"I didn't think my parents even had a sense of humor," Lulu responded honestly.

"They don't, dear. And the only camera in this house is a 1953 Polaroid Land Camera for which they stopped making film. So unfortunately, your dreams of national embarrassment are over. Please mourn silently," Mrs. Wellington said while stopping in front of Lulu.

"Name?"

"Lulu Punchalower."

Mrs. Wellington nodded and sauntered over to Garrison.

"Name?"

"Garrison Feldman."

Mrs. Wellington again nodded and proceeded on to Madeleine.

"Name?"

"Madeleine Masterson."

Mrs. Wellington again nodded and turned toward Theo; however, before she could ask his name, he told her.

"Hello, my name is Theo Bartholomew, and I was wondering if I could call my mom. I'm really concerned. What if she ran out of gas, got into a car accident, or picked up a deranged hitchhiker? I need to get to a phone as soon as possible."

Mrs. Wellington locked eyes with Theo, her bright pink lips turning dark crimson.

"Wow, your lips change colors," Theo unwisely said aloud.

"I was born with an exceptionally high number of capillaries in my lips. They are rather wide and close to the surface, allowing those around me to see them blush, if you will, when embarrassed or, more aptly, annoyed."

"Are you embarrassed?" Theo asked sincerely.

"What in Heaven's name do I have to be embarrassed about?"

"I don't know, maybe your makeup," Theo said earnestly. "All I know is, you haven't known me long enough to be annoyed. My brothers say it takes over a year to fully comprehend how annoying I am."

"Clearly, I am an exceptionally fast learner as I can already tell that you are annoying, with a capital A, or maybe just a capital everything. Oh forget it; I am too annoyed to even explain how annoying you are. . . ."

While Theo may have been annoying, the foursome was beginning to realize that Mrs. Wellington might be more than a tad batty.

CHAPTER 10

EVERYONE'S AFRAID OF SOMETHING:

Lachanophobia is the fear of

vegetables.

C ontestants, contestants, please listen," Mrs. Wellington announced to Lulu, Theo, Madeleine, and
Garrison.

"What did you call us?" Lulu asked confrontationally.

"Contestants. Is English not your first language,
Lulu?"

"Of course, but we're not contestants, we're students."

"Well, if you insist English is your first language,

perhaps it simply isn't your best subject, because you are definitely a contestant."

"No, I'm not."

"Yes, Lulu, you most certainly are."

"All right, then what am I a contestant in?" Lulu asked with raised eyebrows and a self-assured smirk.

"In the beauty pageant of life, you silly little freckle-faced girl," Mrs. Wellington continued as if it were the most obvious of answers.

"Life is not a beauty pageant," Lulu responded.

"Then why am I wearing lipstick?"

Lulu stared at Mrs. Wellington, dumbfounded by her rationale.

"A beauty queen is always prepared," Mrs. Wellington said, answering her own question, or so she thought. "Now then, you children must be famished. And a hungry contestant is soon to be a grumpy one, so leave your bags here; Schmidty will handle them after lunch. Follow me and don't touch anything. I don't take kindly to dirty hands," Mrs. Wellington said as she led the students past the stairway to the start of the Great Hall.

A wave of weakness passed through the children's knees. They had never seen anything of such grandeur and peculiarity in all their lives. The Great Hall was at least three hundred feet long and fifteen feet wide with a high arched ceiling. Thick gold-and-white stripes decorated the walls along with elaborate black wrought-iron sconces. At the very end of the hall was a floor-to-ceiling stained glass window of a young woman adorned with a crown and sash.

However, most notably, there was an infinite array of one-of-a-kind doors flowing from the floor to the walls to the ceiling, each distinctive in size, material, and design. A mere inch from the threshold on the floor was the first door, crafted out of an open-faced pocket watch. It ticked loudly, echoing through the expansive hall. Much as a musician does with a metronome, Mrs. Wellington aligned her steps to the tick of the secondhand. Lulu watched the old woman closely, noticing that not only did she walk to the beat of the clock, but she blinked to it.

With her eyes still plastered to Mrs. Wellington, Lulu was the first to speak. "Um, what's the point?"

"What do you mean?" Mrs. Wellington asked sweetly.

"What's with the strange doors? Do they all lead somewhere?"

"Everything leads somewhere. Haven't you figured

that out by now?" Mrs. Wellington said as they passed a four-by-four-foot door suspended in the middle of the wall.

It had a copper knob so imposing it would take three strapping men just to open it. While the students stared at the giant doorknob, Mrs. Wellington stopped in front of a chalkboard door complete with erasers and a chalk tray. While eight feet high, the chalkboard door was only two feet wide. The special, grilled cheese sandwiches, was written vertically in bright pink chalk. Mrs. Wellington opened the door and slid through sideways into the formal dining room.

"Please suck in your bellies; hefty contestants have been known to get stuck," Mrs. Wellington advised while looking directly at Theo.

Lulu pushed past the others and followed the old dame into the room. Garrison immediately trailed Lulu, and Theo graciously allowed Madeleine to go ahead of him. While Madeleine thought Theo a well-mannered boy, the truth was far more self-serving; he didn't want anyone to see him suck in his belly.

The décor of the dining room was best described as

that of a grandmother's house. It was formal, dated, and extremely worn down by the passage of time. Three paintings of English bulldogs decorated the mint green walls. Oversized golden candelabras, covered in wax and dust, stood at the heads of the formally set table just below a crooked chandelier. Pink and white rose-patterned china sat atop the lace tablecloth.

"This is the dining hall. I'm sure it's much nicer a room than you are used to eating in, but don't fret, I've Scotchgarded the walls in case of any food fights. Not that I am encouraging that, because I certainly am not. Or if I am encouraging it, I am also denying that I am doing so."

Lulu ignored Mrs. Wellington's remark on slinging food and focused on the obvious. "The table is only set for seven. What about the other students?" she asked loudly.

"The cats eat outside due to the strange aroma of their cuisine. I describe it as liver and barbecue sauce with a splash of garlic. I find it terribly unappetizing, but you are more than welcome to sample it yourselves."

"Not the cats, the other human students," Lulu said

while watching Mrs. Wellington closely. "Please tell me there are other people here. . . ."

"Ms. . . ."

"Punchalower."

"Of course, Lulu. I am happy to inform you that there are no other contestants. This summer it will be very, very cozy — just the four of you," Mrs. Wellington said with a wink at Lulu.

"What? But the brochure had all those kids running around," Garrison said with shock. "I was counting on others!"

"That is what you'd call false advertising. Perhaps when the summer is finished you'll write a letter to the board of camps to complain. And please do not let the board's hypothetical status deter you," Mrs. Wellington said.

Theo was dismayed that not only had Mrs. Wellington winked at Lulu, but her lips didn't shift in color at all when speaking to Garrison. Maybe she only disliked him.

"Now then, back to the dining hall. Meals are served at eight AM, twelve PM, and six PM. The crows caw eight times at eight AM, twelve times at twelve PM, and six times at six PM. They are a bell tower of sorts. As long as you know how to count, there shouldn't be much confusion," Mrs. Wellington said with an eye on Garrison.

"What? I know how to count," he mumbled defensively.

"Good, perhaps you can do that for the talent section of the pageant," Mrs. Wellington said to Garrison before turning to the others. "We take after-dinner tea and dessert in the drawing room, but all other food must be consumed in here. As you see, the walls are decorated with Mac's predecessors, Milk, Cookies, and most recently Cheese. Poor little Cheese," Mrs. Wellington blustered while looking at the chocolate brown bulldog stoically posed in the portrait. "Very sad, very sad indeed. Let's all bow our heads in mourning for a moment, and then you may take your seats."

After a few seconds, Mrs. Wellington lifted her head and dabbed her red eyes with a delicate lace handkerchief.

"I'll check on Schmidty and Mac in the kitchen."

Mrs. Wellington passed through an oval archway with

a beaded curtain that led to the kitchen. The children eyed the table, noticing a sterling silver bowl with the name "Macaroni" on it. Before they could exchange any sort of meaningful glances, Mrs. Wellington stormed back into the room, assuming her seat at the head of the table.

"The food shall be arriving momentarily. Please place your napkins on your laps and all elbows off the table," Mrs. Wellington instructed, sitting abnormally straight in her chair. "Beauty queens never slouch," she continued with a glance at Lulu. Madeleine waited for the old woman to look her way, but she didn't. Adding insult to injury, Lulu didn't even appreciate the compliment, mouthing "whatever" in response.

Schmidty carried six plates of grilled cheese and tomato sandwiches to the table with the aptitude of an experienced waiter. Shortly after placing the plates in front of Mrs. Wellington and the children, he pulled out Macaroni's chair. The dog leaped with astounding agility, especially considering his tremendous girth. Once seated atop the chair, Macaroni devoured his kibble, spraying droplets of drool over a three-foot radius.

"Not to be impolite, Mrs. Wellington, but does Macaroni always dine at the table?" Madeleine asked meekly.

"Yes, of course. Why ever would you ask such a thing?" Mrs. Wellington screeched, clearly conveying her deep offense.

"I think she meant that dogs usually eat on the floor, since they're dogs," Theo blurted out.

"And?" Mrs. Wellington asked incredulously.

"Dogs are dumb. They don't mind eating off the floor," Garrison explained.

"Garrison, you yourself seem a bit, how should I say, slow. Perhaps you would like to take your food on the floor," Mrs. Wellington said with bloodred lips.

"Look, lady, just 'cause I'm big and good at sports doesn't mean I'm dumb. I'm at least as smart as these wimps," Garrison responded boorishly.

"Did you just call your classmates wimps, Garrison?"

"Yes, but I didn't mean it. It just slipped out. . . ."

"Young man, I know quite a few wimps, as you put it, who know how to swim. If you continue with such language, I will get you a waterbed. Or perhaps just drop your bed in water with you strapped to it," Mrs. Wellington said with dark cherry-colored lips.

Theo ignored Mrs. Wellington's threat as he thrust the sandwich into his mouth. The young boy's eyes immediately crossed with repulsion. It was hands down the most putrid-tasting grilled cheese sandwich in the world.

"Theo, is there a problem?" Mrs. Wellington asked while staring at the boy's contorted face.

"My tongue," Theo gasped. "The taste buds are rotting."

Lulu rolled her eyes at Theo, then took a bite of her sandwich. Garrison and Madeleine followed suit before Lulu was able to gag in horror.

"What is that, old man?" Lulu howled at Schmidty.

"Lulu, he can't hear. He's deaf and fat. However, the fatness is not the reason for the deafness; I asked the doctor to make sure. You see, for a while it seemed as if there was nowhere left for the fat to go except his ear canals. He had literally filled up every extra inch with chunk. So naturally, I assumed the fat had clogged his ears."

"Madame, your knowledge of the human body is truly astounding," Schmidty added with a huff.

"My tongue. I'm not sure it will ever be the same," Theo moaned. "Without food, I've got nothing. I've already been separated from my family and now . . . food."

"Mr. Theo, I presume you don't care for the Casu Frazigu?" Schmidty said.

"I must need an earbud because I thought I heard you say Casu Frazigu," Madeleine said to Schmidty.

"An earbud," Lulu mocked Madeleine.

"Excuse me, Lulu, but I speak the Queen's English."

"So what? I speak the President's English."

"Yes, and I have a feeling I know exactly which president," Madeleine responded.

"Um, um," Schmidty cleared his throat, "you do not need an earbud or Q-tip. I did indeed say Casu Frazigu. It's Madame's favorite taste, but after the Italian Government made it illegal, I spent years perfecting the flavor through spices and roots and a few secret substances."

"For clarification's sake, there is no actual Casu Frazigu in this sandwich?" Madeleine said while turning green with nausea. Depending on his answer, the table could easily be covered in vomit in seconds.

"No," Schmidty responded.

"What on Earth is this ca-si dra-g-oo?" Theo blubbered with his tongue still hanging out of his mouth.

"Maggot cheese," Madeleine blurted out.

"Maggot cheese!" Lulu screamed.

"I don't understand what that even means," Garrison said honestly. "Cheese comes from cows."

"Yes, Garrison, but when the cheese maker ages it, he allows flies to lay eggs in the cheese. Then maggots," Madeleine said before pausing out of grossness, "are born and swim through the cheese, releasing enzymes which make it taste like . . ."

"Like the most heavenly thing on earth. That's why I have chosen to have all the meals flavored to taste like Casu Frazigu," Mrs. Wellington said happily.

"This could ruin food forever," Theo said dramatically as he placed a piece of gum in his mouth. "I should have gone to fat camp. At least the little food they give you there is good."

"Before anyone continues eating, we must say grace," Mrs. Wellington said while straightening her wig.

"Mrs. Wellington, I should tell you I have an uncertain relationship with God right now," Theo rambled. "It's part of my whole fear-of-death thing. What's going to happen to me? Where will I go? Will I go anywhere? Is it like when I'm asleep? Is it possible that I am already dead and this is all happening in my mind?"

"That's quite enough. Grace has nothing to do with religion in this house. Schmidty, will you please begin before Theo gets another word in?"

Schmidty patted his long gray comb-over before lifting his left hand toward the table display of flowers and greenery. He knocked three times, resulting in a hollow echo, before spouting a quick, "Thank you, Grace."

Mrs. Wellington turned to Garrison, impressing her desire for him to follow Schmidty's lead. He wiped a blond lock off his forehead, then tapped the display three times and casually uttered, "Gracias, Grace."

"I'm afraid Grace doesn't speak Spanish, Garrison," Mrs. Wellington said with a straight face.

"Thank you, Grace," he relented.

Madeleine, Lulu, and Mrs. Wellington followed, leaving just Theo.

"Are you ready? Or are you still in the midst of an existential crisis, Theo?" Mrs. Wellington asked with her lips' color flickering rapidly, unsure what mood to embrace.

Theo stretched his plump white arm toward the display and knocked three times before saying, "Thank you, Grace."

"Was that witchcraft or something? Because I don't want to be involved in that, Mrs. Wellington," Lulu announced.

"Witchcraft?" Mrs. Wellington laughed uproariously. "You have quite the imagination, my pious one. Schmidty prepares all our meals, so it's only appropriate we thank Grace for saving his life and allowing him to continue to cook."

"If I may inquire, who was Grace? And what does she have to do with the table display?" Madeleine asked between sips of orange juice. None of the children touched the sandwiches again.

"Schmidty used to be a risk taker, and I'm not just talking about his hair. I am referring to something much more treacherous . . ." Mrs. Wellington said with a pause worthy of a horror story, ". . . the Lost Forest."

Lulu rolled her eyes and sighed. Theo on the other hand was rapt, utterly seduced by the word "treacherous." Any kind of danger made Theo's ears perk up. He insisted on being aware of the risks around him, in order to take the necessary precautions.

"As I'm sure you've heard, the forest is legendary for

its abilities to confound and confuse even the strongest of men, who become so turned around they never manage to escape. Or perhaps they get stuck in sticky vines with no viable means of extrication. Regardless, many a man, woman, and pet have disappeared in there, but not our Schmidty. He would traipse through the forest to fish the banks of the Moon River, totally oblivious of any danger from the forest to the violent currents."

Garrison's face contorted with fear at the mere mention of the river.

"How did Schmidty get down to the forest?" Madeleine asked.

"I attached the crane to the back of his overalls. But then they ripped, and he plummeted the last twenty feet, breaking both arms. It was such a tragedy; those overalls were quite complimentary on his body, and trust me, that is no simple feat."

"What does any of this have to do with saying Grace?" Garrison asked with agitation, unable to shake the image of a gushing river.

"Patience, my sweaty boy," Mrs. Wellington said with a glance at Garrison's perspiration-covered face. "One day while fishing, the old man fell in. It was simply ghastly, his whole comb-over washed before his eyes. I wish you could ask him about it; he'd do a much better job, but that's the tragedy of the deaf."

"Madame, I am more than capable of telling the story."

"Oh, very well," Mrs. Wellington responded, as if suddenly aware of his hearing capabilities.

"Madame often forgets that I am visually impaired, but my hearing is just fine. As for the story, Madame was quite a fan of the trout, so I often fished on the edge of Moon River."

"Schmidty, I certainly hope you aren't implying it was my fault?"

"Of course not, Madame. I am merely insinuating it was your fault. I think that's the least I could do after your comb-over comment."

"Very well then, please continue."

"As I was saying, I was fishing at the edge of the river, standing on what appeared to be a large rock, but of course, my vision does not lend itself to details. Every few minutes the rock moved under the pressure of the currents, but I paid it no mind. The slight pull on my

fishing line absorbed my attention, as the rock continued to move from the left to the right. I readjusted my
feet while remaining focused on the fishing line. Then
the rock moved out from beneath me, tossing me headfirst into the river. My body was pulled underwater and
the currents wouldn't let me surface. I was dying."

"This is a horrible story," Theo fussed, dabbing mois-
ture from his eyes, "even worse than that sandwich."

"Clearly he didn't die. A little emotional control
would do you good," Mrs. Wellington said firmly.

"I appreciate your concern, Mr. Theo. It's not often
that people show such emotion toward me," Schmidty
said while staring at Mrs. Wellington. "Now then. Where
was I?"

"You were drowning," Madeleine offered helpfully
before noticing the veritable river gushing from Garrison's forehead. She considered telling the old man to
quit the drowning story, but she thought it impolite. Instead, she stared longingly at Garrison to convey her
heartfelt sympathy.

"Buried beneath the water, I spotted a large green
rock swimming toward me. It swam around me until I
grabbed on. Then it pulled me ashore. I was unbelievably

grateful, although I wondered if I was hallucinating, especially since the green rock was following me home. Once Madame saw the rock I learned it was actually a turtle —"

Mrs. Wellington interrupted Schmidty excitedly, "I named her Grace, and once I showed her to the large tub, well, she never left. I didn't mind; she did save Schmidty after all. If he had died who would have cooked my food to taste of Casu Frazigu or laundered my clothes?"

"Thank you, Madame. Your concern is overwhelming."

Mrs. Wellington glanced at Schmidty before reaching toward the centerpiece. "We've kept her shell as a nice reminder of the turtle who used to live in the downstairs bathroom."

"That's a dead turtle shell we knocked on?" Lulu questioned Mrs. Wellington.

"Yes, dear, it is."

"Some turtles have salmonella. Do you realize what that can do to us? I think I feel a fever coming on," Theo said while touching his forehead.

"Grace didn't have salmonella," Mrs. Wellington said calmly. "I had Schmidty lick her shell to confirm it."

"It's true, Mr. Theo. Nary a chill, fever, or nausea."

"It was a very productive activity, as we learned saliva is a good stand-in for furniture polish," Mrs. Wellington said with a straight face.

Garrison, desperate to erase thoughts of rivers and saliva from his mind, focused on the dense garden outside. His eyes were lingering between an elm and maple tree, when he saw something move. Perhaps it was the gardener. He narrowed his eyes to decipher the figure before asking, "Is there anyone else up here?"

"We are all alone up here. Aren't we, Schmidty?" Mrs. Wellington responded with a wry smile.

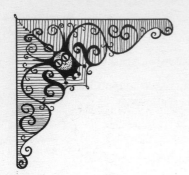

EVERYONE'S AFRAID OF SOMETHING:

Peladophobia is the fear of

bald people.

The children followed Mrs. Wellington and Schmidty into the kitchen, where they placed their plates on the neon pink counter. In a rather unconventional move, Mrs. Wellington had the kitchen done entirely in pink. In addition to the walls, floor, and ceiling, every appliance, plate, utensil, bowl, glass, and tea towel were a shade of pink. The color scheme reminded Garrison of Pepto-Bismol. Theo didn't mind the color so much as the idea of Schmidty in it.

"Isn't it *dangerous* for a blind man to cook?" Theo asked logically.

"Safety is relative. If he can operate the crane, I'm sure he can boil water. He hasn't hurt anyone yet. Well, actually, that's not true. I should say, he hasn't killed anyone," Mrs. Wellington said as her lips dipped a shade darker before returning to normal. "Now then, it's time for your first class. Follow me."

Mrs. Wellington pushed open the ten-foot-by-ten-foot pink Formica accordion door, which led into the Great Hall. The foursome followed Mrs. Wellington, once again awestruck by their surroundings. There were literally more doors than they could count, each more unique than the last. A glass door with a bronze plaque informing residents to use the stairs in case of a fire caught the foursome's attention. A tangled web of staircases crisscrossed the room both vertically and horizontally, creating an indecipherable mess.

Mrs. Wellington, oblivious to the children's interest, continued marching down the hall. "Stop dawdling," Mrs. Wellington announced firmly.

Madeleine, still planted in front of the glass door, sensed something familiar in the midst of the great mess. Her stomach churned loudly as the reality dawned on her. The tightly packed center with long tendrils resembled a gargantuan spider. Madeleine imagined the hairy, multi-legged creature approaching, fangs dripping with poison. Out of habit, she grabbed her repellents and sprayed the glass door.

"What are you doing?" Garrison whispered harshly from a few feet away.

The sound of his voice snapped Madeleine back to reality.

"Sorry, I don't know what came over me," Madeleine replied with embarrassment.

Mrs. Wellington abruptly stopped in front of a traditional red door with a white porch and a wooden rocking chair. It was the sort of quaint setting that inspired people to move to the country.

"I suppose since we're here, I'll show you the B&B. Outside of the library, the Fearnasium, and the classroom, you are not to open any other doors, ever, under any circumstance, real or imagined."

"I love B&Bs," Madeleine chirped.

"You would," Lulu snorted.

"Oh Lulu, you are a funny one," Mrs. Wellington said

with a smile. "And as such, you can enter the B&B first."

"Great," Lulu offered with her trademark eye roll.

Madeleine steamed a little over Mrs. Wellington's oblivion to Lulu's utter lack of gratitude and manners. The old woman almost seemed to like her more because of it.

Garrison, completely bored by the prospect of seeing the B&B, focused on the bulletin board next to the red door. Amid the clutter of old flyers, everything from guitar lessons to the town fair, he spotted a missing-child poster. It was old and frayed, but the photograph of the child was still clear. Just as Garrison prepared to ask the old woman what happened to the boy, she looked over at him purposefully and spoke.

"I tend to keep the B&B rather dim, so it may take your eyes a second to adjust."

"Oh dear, spiders love darkness," Madeleine mumbled while covering herself in repellent.

"Excuse me, Mrs. Wellington. By any chance, is the Bed & Breakfast open for brunch?" Theo asked.

Ignoring Theo, Mrs. Wellington ushered the children, led by Lulu, into the B&B.

"And now for the B&Bs," Mrs. Wellington said while opening a closet.

The onslaught was fast, furious, and unbelievably loud. All they saw were swathes of black, and all they heard was the flapping of wings. Before the foursome could focus their eyes on the black masses storming around their heads, Mrs. Wellington lifted the top of a massive urn, releasing a strong and focused stream of bees. The buzzing was thunderous, even as the flapping sounds continued.

"Bats and bees," Mrs. Wellington said jubilantly as the foursome cowered in a huddle.

"Bats!" Lulu screamed in shock before throwing open the front door.

"I've been stung," Theo yelled while following Lulu.

Madeleine was last out after Garrison, leaving Mrs. Wellington alone with the B&Bs.

"They're all over me!" Madeleine hollered while spraying furiously.

Garrison, sensing the girl's hysteria, grabbed her arms and shook her for a second.

"There is nothing on you," he said calmly while using his right hand to flick one lone bee from her shoulder.

"Were those African killer bees?" Theo said with tears in his eyes.

"Oh Heavens no, Theo," Mrs. Wellington said while exiting the B&B, her entire wig engulfed in bees.

"Lady, your whole head is covered in bees," Lulu said while staring at the old woman.

A small black face popped over Mrs. Wellington's shoulder and flapped its wings.

"There's also one ugly bat on your back," Garrison said while stepping away.

"Oh, that's Harriet. She is such a naughty little thing. She is always trying to escape, just loves the light." Mrs. Wellington grabbed Harriet and tossed her back into the B&B.

"Why do you have bats and bees?" Theo mumbled.

"Oh, it's not always bees and bats. Sometimes it's birds and barracudas, black widows and blue crabs, or black-footed ferrets and boa constrictors. It simply depends on which doors or containers you open. But not to worry — the B&B is theoretically sealed."

"Did you say *theoretically* sealed? And black widows? I don't feel so well," Madeleine moaned.

"A theoretic seal is virtually airtight, absolutely nothing to fear," Mrs. Wellington said confidently. "Now then, on to the classroom."

"But your head," Madeleine said while spraying madly, "it's still completely covered in bees."

"It's the shampoo I use, lavender honey," Mrs. Wellington said as she removed her bee-covered wig and tossed it inside the B&B.

The foursome gasped as they stared at her old and wrinkled bald head.

Mrs. Wellington pulled another bob wig from her jacket and placed it on her head.

"Not to worry, contestants, a beauty queen is always prepared."

At this point, the foursome wondered if *they* were prepared for what they would encounter at the strange school.

CHAPTER 12

EVERYONE'S AFRAID OF SOMETHING:

Nomatophobia is the fear of

names.

Once back in the Great Hall, the students passed farm gates, portions of an airplane, and much more before arriving at massive double white doors with ostentatious gold leafed detail. The ballroom was vast, grand, and altogether spectacular. The children squinted as they took in the two parts of the sun-filled room. To the right was the drawing room, a neatly arranged sitting area with four charcoal gray armchairs and two matching sofas, and to the left was the classroom.

Traditionally, children's classrooms contain wooden chairs, dull brown desks, and maybe a poster or two, but not at School of Fear. Mrs. Wellington instead filled the classroom with twenty silver-leafed student desks and matching chairs. Ten rows, consisting of two desks each, descended in size. The last row featured regular child-size desks and chairs, with the row in front slightly smaller and so on. By the first row, the desks were so small that only squirrels could sit at them comfortably. Theo eyed the desks with his customary suspicion.

"Is there lead in this paint? Metallic paints can be extremely high in lead, which is very dangerous to kids."

"Thank you, Captain Safety, for the tutorial on lead paint. I assure you, the only danger associated with these desks is that of a concussion."

"I've had a lot of concussions," Garrison said, reminiscing about his many days on the soccer, baseball, and football fields. "Most *great* athletes have."

"*Someone* thinks pretty highly of himself," Lulu said beneath her breath.

"Shut it, freckleface," Garrison snapped back.

"Whatever, at least I know how to swim."

"Stop talking," Theo interrupted loudly. "I need to

hear about the concussions. Does the paint make you cloudy headed, then you trip and fall?"

"Oh, no. It's a great deal simpler. When I toss the small desks at contestants, they sometimes get concussions," Mrs. Wellington said genuinely.

"You throw desks," Theo said incredulously, "at our heads? You know, where we keep our brains?"

"In England, throwing desks at children is strictly forbidden," Madeleine reported.

"I prefer to think of my methods as 'highly unconventional' rather than 'strictly forbidden,' as you say," Mrs. Wellington said unemotionally.

"So you have the small desks just to throw at us?" Garrison asked with disdain.

"It's a bit more scientific than that. The height and weight of a child influences their fear. For instance, many petite children feel dwarfed by big furniture. Small desks allow them to feel big and strong. It's a confidence-building exercise."

"Except when you throw the desks at their heads," Lulu added.

"You certainly are a sharp one," Mrs. Wellington said to Lulu with what seemed to be sincerity.

"I know," Lulu said with obvious self-satisfaction.

This time it was Madeleine who rolled her eyes.

"Please take a seat, but choose prudently, as I loathe seat changes. It messes terribly with my memory. In all honesty, I would prefer you wear the same outfits every day," she continued while leaning against her elaborate teacher's desk, "but in the past it has led to rather foul odors, so instead I shall simply ask you to stay at the same desk for the duration of the summer."

"We could wear name tags," Madeleine offered earnestly.

"Name tags are even more ghastly than calling you the wrong name. This isn't a convention center," Mrs. Wellington huffed.

Madeleine was sure that if Lulu had suggested name tags, Mrs. Wellington would have loved the idea. Irritated, she decided to focus on fumigating her desk in the far right corner. Garrison, tired of the sting of repellent in his nostrils, chose a seat in the row in front of Madeleine. Theo sat next to Madeleine, and Lulu next to Garrison.

"Fiona? Errol?" Mrs. Wellington called out cheerfully.

The cats ignored her, never once stirring from their spot of sunshine on the shiny parquet floor.

"Incredible. Such training," Mrs. Wellington said dramatically. "I would like to begin with a simple exercise — tell me your fear. Let's start with the beekeeper in the back."

Madeleine stared blankly at Mrs. Wellington, apparently unaware that she resembled a beekeeper.

"Come on, darling, you in the safari garb, let's go."

"Oh, me? I am petrified of spiders, bugs, insects, and any mixture of the three."

"Mrs. Wellington, I'd like to share some pertinent information with the group. In 2003 twenty people died from insect and spider bites," Theo explained.

"Yes, that sounds about right. I lost a cousin to a black widow bite that very year."

"Your cousin died?" Madeleine gasped.

"Well, of course he died. What did you think I meant? I lost him in the park? Honestly, Madeleine," Mrs. Wellington said, shaking her head. "My portly friend, it's your turn."

Theo responded without pause.

"I'm scared of my family dying. Or me dying. Death

145

in general. And along those lines, anything dangerous or worrisome I try my best to avoid. I think of it as being safety-conscious."

"For the record, dying doesn't interest me much either. Sporty?"

"I kick butt at soccer, baseball, and basketball."

"Dear boy, this isn't an athletic camp. . . ."

Garrison sighed, looked at his desk, and whispered, "I'm afraid of water — pools, lakes, rivers, oceans."

"In 2003 3,306 people died from drowning," Theo interjected confidently.

"And the young lady rolling her eyes back in her head, what are you afraid of?" Mrs. Wellington asked Lulu.

"I'm claustrophobic, which is a fancy way of saying I'm terrified of confined spaces. Let's just say I really like windows."

"I don't have all confined space statistics, but I know that in 2003, forty-six people died due to cave-ins," Theo said seriously, "which is sort of related, since I think the cave-ins happened in small spaces."

"Why are you sharing all these horrible statistics?" Lulu screamed.

"And why are all your facts from 2003? Don't you have anything more recent?" Garrison snapped.

"2003 is the latest National Safety Council book my library has," Theo murmured.

As if oblivious to the quarrel, Mrs. Wellington responded to Lulu's claustrophobia. "I once got stuck in an elevator for twenty-six hours. It was so crowded I couldn't move more than two inches in any direction."

"Did you use the emergency phone?" Lulu asked.

"Oh, how much you have to learn. Those phones are for decoration, like a painting on a wall or a stop sign in the street," Mrs. Wellington said before pausing to remember the traumatic incident. "All sixteen of us thought we were going to die, standing up, which is not the way you want to go. If ever given a choice, always choose to die lying down. Of course, we didn't have this option, since it was so crowded. I must say those twenty-six hours brought us together. We used to meet once a year at the annual Not Just Yet event, but . . ."

"The Not Just Yet event?" Lulu asked doubtfully.

"It was a wonderful society of people, bound together by the common experience of almost dying. Most of the members were recruited following newspaper stories or occasionally even in the emergency room."

"Excuse me, Mrs. Wellington," Lulu asked assertively, "what are your credentials?"

"Yes, I am rather curious where you learned this particular curriculum," Madeleine concurred.

"A beauty queen is always prepared, and that includes knowing her résumé by heart. Now then, I was Miss Teen USA, Miss Massachusetts, Miss New England, Miss Green County, and of course Miss Summerstone. Didn't you see the pictures downstairs? I would display my crowns, but we have had incidents of theft in the past. Mostly Schmidty borrowing them, but still."

"I meant your credentials to *teach* us!" Lulu said loudly.

"Oh, you silly girl! Teachers don't need credentials. That's an old wives' tale."

"So you have absolutely no valid credentials to teach us about fears," Madeleine said in shock.

"I assure you that one doesn't need credentials for fears when one has a Fearnasium."

"A what?" Garrison asked.

"A gymnasium for exercising fears."

"Exercise, whether physical or mental, real or imaginary, is a very important part of the day," Mrs. Wellington announced as she unlocked the faded plywood door that led to the Fearnasium.

"Are there treadmills and weights? 'Cause I'd like to stay in good shape while I'm here," Garrison asked Mrs. Wellington.

"I'm afraid not, Sporty."

Garrison sighed and looked away as Mrs. Wellington pulled open the door.

Approximately half the size of a basketball court with a shiny wooden floor, the room could easily have passed for a regular gymnasium. It was the contents of the room that greatly set it apart. An entire wall was devoted to leather-bound books, each covering a different phobia, everything from acarophobia to zelmmiphobia. Upon sight of the books, Madeleine felt a bit better, more at ease. If Mrs. Wellington had read all these books, she must know something.

"Are the books properly secured in case of an earthquake?" Theo asked.

"We don't have earthquakes in Massachusetts."

"Actually in 1965 . . ."

"Stop right there, my chubby fact finder. The event you are referring to was not an earthquake. It was more of a hiccup or belch, but definitely not an earthquake."

"And you've read all those books," Madeleine asked hopefully.

"'Read' is a strong word. I prefer 'scanned,' 'perused,' 'osmoted' . . ."

"Osmoted?" Madeleine inquired.

"Oh yes, that's when you garner information through osmosis. It's very scientific."

Outside of the wall of books, the room was rather peculiar-looking, with multiple booths, each dedicated to a different fear. There was a fire booth, where one would sit in a temporized glass box as flames erupted around it. There were life-size dolls, clowns, science fiction-esque creatures, bubbling pots of tar, buckets of simulated vomit, a quicksand sandbox, a massive ant farm, an aquarium filled with creepy critters from the sea, a knife block, puppets, a bathtub, a coffin, stuffed animals, vats of cough syrup, barrels of glass eyes, skeletons, a dentist's chair, a high school cafeteria table, needles, and much more.

"Mrs. Wellington? Has that been used?" Theo said, pointing to the coffin.

"Used? Dear misguided, morbid Chubby, they aren't like toasters you pick up secondhand from a garage sale. They are buried in the ground with dead people. I suppose you could dig them up and remove the dead person, but I imagine the smell to be ghastly."

"What exactly are we going to do in here?" Lulu asked with mounting trepidation as she perused the selection of claustrophobic possibilities.

"For today we'll just do some imaginary exercises."

"Imaginary exercises?" Madeleine asked curiously.

"Yes. If used correctly, imagination can prep you for a great deal of life's hardships. Garrison is to imagine he is submerged in the bathtub, slowly becoming used to the sensation of water. Lulu and Theo are two peas in a pod, or rather coffin, learning to accept confined spaces and mortality. And as for Madeleine, well, you are to embrace being covered in four large and hairy but fake spiders. On the count of three you are to close your eyes and imagine your predicaments."

Each of the four children told themselves that they would do no such thing. They yearned to think of anything other than what Mrs. Wellington had told them to, but oddly the more they tried to resist, the harder it became. By the time Mrs. Wellington said three, Madeleine's body was electrified with fear at the thought of hairy, albeit plastic, spider feet on her arm. Lulu felt a sudden surge behind her left eye as she experienced the breath-stifling darkness of the coffin. Garrison began to sweat as he fought the image of water encapsulating his body. Of course, the more he sweat, the realer it became, damp clothes and all. Theo actually showed the greatest ability to control his mind. Perhaps it was his slightly hysterical personality that allowed him to jump from subject to subject in his mind.

While at first terrified by the thought of being in a coffin, he soon wondered how long he had to go without sunlight before developing rickets. As rickets rhymes with crickets, Theo quickly began thinking about the outbreak of Indonesian crickets that caused flulike symptoms in humans after biting them. Theo had meant to follow up and confirm that there were no other long-term effects to the cricket case, but he forgot. And just like that, the exercise was over.

"Good job, contestants."

"I have a headache," Lulu moaned while covering her left eye with her hand.

"If you hold your hand like that, you could damage your eye, Lulu. Or you could trip and fall," Theo warned, oblivious to the girl's condition.

"I feel a bit weak myself," Madeleine said as she sat down in the dentist chair to ease her nauseated stomach.

Garrison wiped his brow on his sleeve and walked toward a door behind Madeleine and the dentist chair. It was a heavy metal door, similar to that of a vault with a wheel handle. Scratched in nearly illegible marker was "Munchauser's Masterpiece."

"What's Munchauser's Masterpiece?" Garrison asked Mrs. Wellington.

"Oh! That room. That room, what a disappointment. He tried to create a machine to beat the track. No need to go in there, contestants," Mrs. Wellington said while adjusting her wig. "The whole lot of you look exhausted. Come, let me show you to your living quarters. There's nothing to be afraid of there, but don't fret; we'll certainly be returning to the Fearnasium."

That was what worried Lulu, Madeleine, Theo, and Garrison.

CHAPTER 13

EVERYONE'S AFRAID OF SOMETHING:

Ailurophobia is the fear of

cats.

Ratty & Errol

The living quarters, as Mrs. Wellington referred to them, were on Summerstone's second floor, which was a far less imposing setting than the first floor. The children's "quarters" consisted of two rooms connected by a bathroom. First along the hallway was the blue door with the words GARCON, RAGAZZO, BUB, and BOY inscribed on it. Behind the door, blue and white striped wallpaper, hardwood floors, and heavy sun-stained navy curtains surrounded two twin beds with sapphire gingham bedspreads. Above each bed was a painting of Errol and Ratty, the cats, playing baseball in uniforms.

"Sometimes I regret training them to ignore me. It would have been refreshing to have an all-feline base-ball team. Of course, the uniforms would prove a challenge. Ratty and Errol threw such tantrums when they sat for their portraits," Mrs. Wellington said fondly while gazing at the paintings.

A similar set of paintings, starring Fiona and Anna-belle in tutus and toe shoes, hung above the girls' beds. As with the boys' room, FILLE, RAGAZZA, FRAULEIN, and GIRL, in perfect calligraphy, were painted on the door. Upon entering the room, Madeleine immediately real-ized that Mrs. Wellington's love of the color pink was not limited to the kitchen. Soft pink walls with white polka dots clashed with mauve carpet, fuchsia curtains, and cherry-colored paisley duvets.

Madeleine canvassed the corners for cobwebs while haphazardly spraying around her body. As she took note of her own reflection, barely visible beneath the netting she wore, a tinge of sadness passed over her. She quickly snapped out of it, remembering that vanity was a small price to pay to avoid sticky spider feet. The thought of a spider's many legs gave her goose bumps and a whiff of nausea, as did the paisley-print bedspread.

"Mrs. Wellington, when was the last time this room was sprayed for insects by an exterminator?"

"This morning, dear. I sent Schmidty up here with four cans of repellent and told him to spray until he passed out."

"How long did he last?" Madeleine asked in all seriousness.

"I'd say a good forty-five minutes. Macaroni only lasted ten; short-nosed dogs simply don't have the lung capacity for that kind of work."

"And during the extermination, were the blankets and sheets sprayed?"

"No, dear."

"What?" Madeleine gasped frantically.

"Of course not; I had them laundered in a repellent."

"Gross," Lulu moaned. "Did you do it to both beds?"

"Certainly; I didn't want either one of you to feel *trapped*, like you had to sleep in a certain bed," Mrs. Wellington said with emphasis on the word "trapped." Lulu understood what she meant, having long insisted on sleeping as close to a window as possible.

"Thanks," Lulu said in a hushed tone while approaching the window.

Lulu pulled back the grotesque fuchsia curtains and checked the windows' ability to open. Staring blankly into the yard below, she felt a shiver flow up her spine, setting off the twitch behind her left eye. Inexplicably, Lulu had the distinct feeling of being watched, and not by Mrs. Wellington or her classmates. She scanned the yard for eyes, shadows, or movement but saw nothing. Perhaps it was nerves, Lulu thought, turning away from the window.

After spotting the rusty bathroom doorknob, Lulu was able to shake the feeling of eyes following her. Well, technically, she didn't so much shake the feeling as overwhelm it with a more familiar emotion: panic. Lulu was certain that the dilapidated knob could not lock or, more importantly, unlock properly. She stood in front of the bathroom, paralyzed with thoughts of a room without windows. She knew it wasn't a good sign that the bathroom appeared dark. Surely if there was a window, the room would be lighter. Spasms exploded in Lulu's left eye as Mrs. Wellington watched her closely.

"Not to worry, Lulu, the blinds are merely closed in the bathroom. Believe me; the window is large enough to accommodate your body if needed. You will drop two stories and break your legs, but you will live."

"Oh, I wasn't worried," Lulu lied as her heart rate slowed to a normal adolescent speed.

"No reason to play tough, my dear — this is School of Fear after all. If you didn't have a fear, you would have no business being here."

"Yeah, I guess," Lulu responded as her eye stopped twitching.

"Before I leave you, I want to inform you that farther down the hall is the barbershop, Schmidty's room, and my suite. None of these areas are contestant-friendly. In other words, don't bother us unless there's an emergency."

"What if we want a haircut?" Garrison asked snidely.

"The barbershop is a shrine to my husband, who died of a heart attack on the bus up here."

"Oh," Garrison said awkwardly.

"Was he a barber?" Theo asked.

"No, but the last thing he said as he clutched his chest was, 'I wish I had gotten my hair cut.'"

The children silently agreed that the best response to this comment was no response at all.

That night at dinner, Madeleine, Theo, Garrison, and Lulu were delighted to discover that, unbeknownst to Mrs. Wellington, Schmidty had skipped the Casu Frazigu flavoring in their food. Mrs. Wellington, on the other hand, was rather delighted that the foursome had come around so quickly to the delicacy. With a stealth look from Schmidty, everyone understood that what Mrs. Wellington didn't know wouldn't hurt her.

After dinner, Madeleine followed Lulu around their pink bedroom, analyzing the situation. "She seems a bit odd. Perhaps a trifle mad," Madeleine said cautiously.

"I guess," Lulu said.

"Did you happen to see a phone downstairs?" Madeleine asked hopefully.

"Of course. . . ." Lulu trailed off, wondering if she had in fact seen a phone downstairs. "Well, I'm almost certain I did."

In the boys' room, Theo curled up in the fetal position and stared misty-eyed at the wall. Memories of holiday dinners, watching television with his sisters, and logging family check-ins in "Dead or Alive" wafted through his mind. Theo missed his family so much it actually hurt to breathe, or maybe that was because he was in the fetal position and his muscles were cramping. Either way, the boy was in pain.

Theo imagined his poor, old, tired mother hysterical over her decision not to give him a cell phone. Of course, in actuality, his mother was enjoying a late dinner at Elaine's with her husband. As Theo agonized over his mother's misery, Garrison lay on the gingham bedspread reading the only magazine he'd brought. If Garrison had known that the only other boy at the school would be so wimpy, he would have packed a thousand sports magazines, or, better yet, he simply wouldn't have come.

"Do you miss your family?" Theo blustered as the heat from his tears steamed his glasses.

"We haven't even been gone a full day yet," Garrison responded with frustration. "You need to get a grip. Trust me, wherever they are, they are better off than we are with a weird old lady and a blind guy with a combover. It's a statistical fact," Garrison said to Theo.

Theo nodded at Garrison, who then feigned casualness as he asked something that had been on his mind since

Theo started spouting statistics earlier, "By any chance, do you know the likelihood of a tsunami hitting Miami?"

"I don't have exact numbers on tsunamis for that region, but if I were you I would be more worried about hurricanes. I had to miss the class trip to Disney World last year, all because they insisted on scheduling it during prime hurricane season. I'm sorry, but there aren't enough churros in the world to make that worth it."

Garrison nodded his head at Theo, picked up his magazine, and pretended to keep reading. He reminded himself of his escape plan in case of a hurricane warning — book ticket over phone and call parents upon arrival in New York. Just as Garrison stopped perspiring over hypothetical water disasters, there was a soft knock at the bathroom door. Before either Theo or Garrison could respond, Lulu and Madeleine popped their heads into the boys' room.

"Hey, did you guys see a phone downstairs?" Lulu asked casually. "I'm totally fine, but Madeleine is kind of freaking out."

"I most certainly am *not* freaking out, Lulu. In light of Mrs. Wellington's bizarre behavior, I simply would like to know where the phones are located."

Theo jumped off his bed, excitement resonating from every pore in his body.

"Yes, Madeleine," Theo said with delight, "I couldn't agree more. Let's go downstairs and find all the phones and call our parents. I may cry, so bring some tissues. Then, we'll create maps so wherever we are in the house, we will know where the closest phone is."

Madeleine stared at Theo, a bit dumbfounded by his elaborate plan.

"I just meant I would like to know where a phone is. I don't think we need to map it out."

"Hold it," Garrison said authoritatively. "You guys need to chill out. No one is going downstairs and getting us in trouble on our first night. I didn't come all this way to spend my summer in detention."

"Fine, but answer me this," Theo said seriously, "did you see a phone?"

Garrison stared at the three of them and instantly knew what he had to do. Lie.

"Of course I saw a phone. Now everyone go to bed."

And with the knowledge that there was a phone in the house, everyone fell easily to sleep. Well, everyone except Garrison.

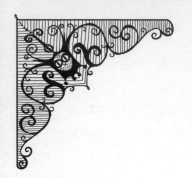

CHAPTER 14

EVERYONE'S AFRAID OF SOMETHING:

Logizomechanophobia is the fear of

computers.

Madeleine longed to see a conservatively stylish bedroom with a globe and a rocking chair when she opened her eyes. Such a refined room would signify that the feet clattering down the hall belonged to her mother and that School of Fear had only been a bizarre dream. However, she knew that even a speck of pink would indicate the continuation of School of Fear. Madeleine took a deep breath before forcing her eyes open.

The obliteration of hope burned through her as she saw that she remained in the pink palace.

A few feet away, strands of Lulu's strawberry blond hair fluttered across her face as she inhaled and exhaled loudly. A familiar voice boomed through the pink door, wrestling Lulu from sleep and Madeleine from thoughts of home.

"Ms. Madeleine, Ms. Lulu, you have fifteen minutes to wash and dress for breakfast. Pay special attention to your teeth. I also encourage the use of mouthwash, as Mrs. Wellington has a terrible aversion to morning breath. She'll scrub your mouth with baking soda and vinegar for the faintest odor."

"Got it, Schmidty," Lulu yelled from her bed before turning toward a morbidly depressed Madeleine. "She's afraid of morning breath? Whatever. I'm afraid of her bald head."

"Oh please, you have nothing to worry about. You're her favorite."

Inside the yellow bathroom with green accents, Lulu discovered two pajama-clad boys with half-open eyes and a dog at their feet. While barely conscious, Theo and Garrison brushed their teeth with fervor.

"What's the dog doing in here?" Lulu asked. "And why's he wearing pajamas?"

"Listen, all I know is I woke up snuggling him," Theo said with a waterfall of toothpaste coming out of his mouth. "Well, actually, Macaroni was snuggling me."

"Stop talking and start brushing," Garrison instructed Lulu. "Hey, Maddie, you better get in here; we have to be down there in less than five minutes."

Hearing Garrison refer to her as "Maddie" buoyed her spirits, prompting Madeleine to join the others in the bathroom. Four small faces reflected in the mirror as the sound of fast-moving bristles filled the room.

The different brushing styles clearly characterized the children's personalities: Madeleine preferred a detailed, albeit slow, technique, cleaning each tooth front and back before continuing down the row. Lulu was more haphazard, shoving the toothbrush all around her mouth at an unproductively fast pace. In a testament to Garrison's strength, he forcefully brushed his tongue while controlling his gag reflex. As for Theo, he reapplied toothpaste to his brush every few seconds. Apparently, he couldn't adhere to the recommended pea-size application.

Minutes later the messily dressed foursome sat at the dining room table, listening to the crows caw eight times. With their palms awkwardly cupped over their mouths, the students attempted to smell their own breath. Unfortunately, it's nearly impossible to experience one's own breath.

Unsure what their second day held, a mild pulsation formed in Lulu's left eye, the start of the twitch. She rubbed her eyes harshly, so intensely that when she opened them, spots of light interrupted her vision. Lulu turned her head toward the window and gasped. A man. An outrageously ugly man was peering through the window. Before Lulu was able to formulate words, a spot of light bounced across her vision, obstructing the man's face.

Unnerved by the situation, Lulu closed her eyes and counted to ten. As she neared the number ten in her mind, she became nervous of either outcome. If he was still there, sheer panic would ensue. Yet if he wasn't, that meant she had imagined him, which was equally terrifying. She slowly opened her eyes, immediately noticing a potted plant in the exact place she had seen the mangled face. Could she have mistaken the potted plant for a man's misshaped face?

"I-I saw . . . ," Lulu stammered before realizing how crazy she would sound. "I, um, was wondering if someone would smell my breath?"

"No way," Garrison responded.

"If absolutely necessary, yes, but I would rather not," Madeleine diplomatically responded.

"Lean in, lady, I'll take a sniff," Theo offered warmly.

"Never mind," Lulu said while staring at Theo's face.

She didn't actually want anyone to smell her breath; it was merely the first question that came to her mind.

"What? I'm not good enough to smell your breath?"

Lulu smirked at Theo as he mouthed the word "mean" back to her.

"I see you've been informed of the morning breath tests," Mrs. Wellington said from the hallway, sporting a seersucker sleeveless dress with a petticoat and a matching pillbox hat.

Mrs. Wellington lapped the table once before leaning over Garrison. "Open wide," Mrs. Wellington said calmly.

Garrison leaned his head back and opened his mouth. He didn't blow air in Mrs. Wellington's face; he simply allowed the woman to smell the general area. Sweat formed on his brow as he worried that he hadn't pushed the toothbrush back far enough on his tongue. It was a delicate job, as too much force could lead to vomit, which never helps one's breath.

Mrs. Wellington pulled her head away from Garrison and slowly inhaled through her nose. Time seemed to stand still as she pondered his breath much as a scientist would lab results. Finally, the old woman nodded. She then adjusted her small seersucker hat and proceeded on to Madeleine. Although the smell of her breath could easily make it through the veil, Madeleine lifted it over her mouth. Mrs. Wellington quickly nodded and proceeded to check Lulu and Theo. Both students received the nod of approval, much to their relief.

"Very good, contestants. Not only is a beauty queen always prepared, she also doesn't converse with foul-breathed people," Mrs. Wellington said as Schmidty and Macaroni entered with a platter of scrambled eggs, muffins, and orange juice. "Open wide, old man."

"Madame, I am not a student of this institution. I hardly think I am subject to such inspections."

"You may not be a contestant, but I am a beauty queen. And what do I always say?"

"Never ask a beauty queen her age?"

"No," Mrs. Wellington responded curtly.

"Always pack an extra wig?"

"No."

"Match your eye shadow to your clothes?"

"Listen here, old man, you know very well that I *always* say that a beauty queen doesn't converse with foul-breathed people."

"If you say so, Madame."

"Good, now open wide."

"Very well, Madame. But I think you should know that I have already ordered the epitaph for your tombstone: 'As unfailingly stylish as she was mad.'"

"Dear man, are you already planning my funeral?"

"Since the day we met."

"I've always admired your foresight."

Schmidty, seated at the table, used one hand to hold his comb-over in place while leaning back.

"Remember, bad breath is a sign that bacteria is still present, and trust me, bacteria is no present."

With a saccharine smile, Mrs. Wellington sniffed the inside of Schmidty's mouth and nodded.

"See how much you've already learned!" Mrs. Wellington said.

"What? To brush our teeth?" Lulu asked sarcastically.

"I am sorry to interrupt, but I think I should call my family to check in. A lot of terrible, horrible, dreadful, awful things could have transpired. So can I use the phone?"

Garrison suddenly began to perspire with worry over his white lie the night before. It was completely logical to assume the mansion had phones, so why was his heart racing?

"Of course, Chubby. You may make as many imaginary calls as you like," Mrs. Wellington said with a smile. "I know how much contestants love to chat."

Garrison breathed a sigh of relief, before realizing Mrs. Wellington had said *imaginary* calls.

"What do you mean by *imaginary* calls?" Garrison asked with mounting perspiration.

"There are no telephone lines on the mountain, so all calls must be kept imaginary."

"But there are phones in the house?" Garrison spat out nervously.

"Oh yes," Mrs. Wellington responded.

"Why do you have phones," Theo asked, "if there are no phone lines?"

"I enjoy the appearance of a phone," Mrs. Wellington said. "Plus occasionally I like to call myself and check in, see how I'm doing emotionally."

"I don't even know what that means," Garrison said while staring at the unusual old woman.

"Do you have a computer or PDA device? You know, a BlackBerry? Sidekick? Something?" Theo asked desperately.

"Absolutely not! No TVs, computers, or phones! The only modern allowances are running water and electricity, and we only have those because the former allows me to wash my wig and the latter to dry it.

"Now, then," Mrs. Wellington said while completely ignoring the children's glum expressions, "While you are here, I would prefer to keep you occupied and myself entertained by spending as much of our time as possible inside the Fearnasium. That is why we're here, isn't it, contestants?"

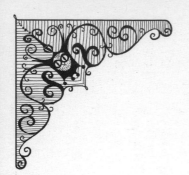

CHAPTER 15

EVERYONE'S AFRAID OF SOMETHING:

Osmophobia is the fear of

smells.

After breakfast, the foursome made a quick stop at the Fearnasium for yet another imaginary exercise, before heading toward the classroom. Madeleine was a bit green again, for despite every intention not to, she had imagined large lifelike spiders all over her arm. Emotionally exhausted, she wished desperately for a pleasant distraction.

"Excuse me, Mrs. Wellington. Yesterday I believe you

referred to a library. While I can't speak for the others, I would very much enjoy the company of a book."

"Oh yes, the library. No school is complete without a library. It's rather conveniently located next to the classroom," Mrs. Wellington said while pointing to a triangle-shaped door.

A shiny copper bell decorated the northernmost tip of the brown triangular door. Due to the small stature of the door, Mrs. Wellington was forced to hunch over and hold her wig as she entered.

While libraries certainly weren't out of the ordinary in mansions as grand as Summerstone, this particular *type* of library was rather unusual. Instead of books neatly placed on the shelves, there were glass jars. Every shelf but one was jammed full of jars. The most potent of all the library's contents sat alone on a bronze-plated shelf near the ceiling.

Inside the various jars were lumps, bumps, and humps of various colors from pink to black, although most resembled the color of an unripe banana, a yellow-ish green.

"What did you do with the books?" Theo implored after scanning the walls.

"Books? This is the Library of Smelly Foods."

"Of what?" Lulu asked with disgust.

"Impressive, isn't it? We have an entire wall dedicated to cheese alone. Then there's clams, gefilte fish, rotten eggs, boiled cabbage, kimchi, sardines, durian fruit, plus all the items that have grown smelly with mold and time. You won't believe how much a tuna sandwich from the bicentennial reeks."

"What's the bicentennial?" Garrison asked.

"It was the two-hundred-year anniversary of the founding of your country," Madeleine said dreamily to Garrison. "It occurred in 1976."

"Honestly, Garrison, she's not even American and *she* knows that," Lulu said condescendingly.

"Oh, like you knew what it was?" Garrison rebuked.

"Guys, just admit that Madeleine is smarter than both of you and move on," Theo said earnestly.

"Smarter than *us*? I hope you aren't insinuating that *you* are smarter than *we* are, Friar Tuck," Lulu said cattily.

"Yeah," Garrison chimed in uselessly. "Wait, who is Friar Tuck?"

"He's Robin Hood's fat, I mean *plump,* friend," Madeleine explained.

"See, she is smarter than you guys," Theo bellowed victoriously.

"No, she's smarter than Garrison," Lulu explained, "not me."

Madeleine sighed loudly before crossing her arms angrily.

"I could wipe the floor with all of you in any sport," Garrison said defensively.

"There should be no wiping or even touching of the floors — they are filled with bacteria," Theo interjected.

"Shut up!" Lulu and Garrison raged in unison.

"There's no need to yell at him," Madeleine said calmly.

"Thank you. Finally, someone who understands me," Theo said theatrically.

Lulu sighed with irritation while rolling her eyes.

"You know the eye muscles are like any other muscle; they get bigger when you exercise them," Theo said.

"Because you know so much about exercise," Lulu said rudely.

"Don't blame me if your eyes bulge out of your head!"

"Theo, enough," Madeleine said while spraying repellent.

"Fine, but I'll have you know that stuff isn't just toxic for the bugs."

"Regret defending him yet?" Lulu asked Madeleine.

Mrs. Wellington remained utterly oblivious on the other side of the library. She was far too enraptured by the various jars to listen to the sparring children. From the tip of her nose, she inspected the finely typed label on the top of each jar. After squinting heavily, Mrs. Wellington relented and put on her tortoiseshell glasses.

"Gather round," Mrs. Wellington said, pushing her glasses up the bridge of her nose. Lulu, Garrison, Madeleine, and Theo inched closer to Mrs. Wellington to inspect the strange brown substance in the jar. Lulu stood perfectly still as her left eye pulsated and bulged with stress. Irrationally, Lulu empathized with the foreign substance, imagining herself in miniature, confined to the jar.

Mrs. Wellington tried to twist off the top. She turned and turned but nothing happened. Her face contorted and her knuckles flashed white as she battled to open the jar.

"This . . . is . . . a . . . tricky fellow . . . ," Mrs. Wellington uttered between breaths. "It's . . . all . . . the . . . gases . . . that . . . form . . . over . . . time."

"I hope the gas isn't flammable," Theo said.

"Does anyone have a match?" Lulu offered snidely while staring down Theo.

"Al . . . most . . . there . . . ," Mrs. Wellington huffed.

"Fire safety is nothing to laugh about, *Lulu*," Theo ranted.

"Loo means toilet in England," Madeleine offered absentmindedly.

"That is *not* true," Lulu yelled at Madeleine, instantly flustering the girl behind the veil.

"I am going to call you Toilet Toilet!" Theo bellowed with laughter.

"Don't you dare, chubs!"

Lulu pushed up her sleeves, prepared to slap Theo if he said one more thing. Madeleine lowered her head in regret, wondering why she had chosen that moment to share such information. And Garrison wondered if he should offer to help the old woman with the jar.

"Got it!" Mrs. Wellington screamed as the top popped off.

The wretched odor exploded into the room, destroying the olfactory senses of all the students. Their eyes crossed, their knees weakened, and their throats constricted. It was the single most offensive aroma they had ever experienced; a ghastly combination of feet, cow manure, vomit, and babies' diapers.

Mrs. Wellington appeared oblivious to the smell, while Theo dry-heaved loudly. Across Madeleine's left and right feet were the bodies of two cats who had literally fainted from the stench. Lulu's left eye pulsated harshly as she moved toward the door. Garrison pulled his shirt over his mouth and followed Lulu to the Great Hall.

Once in the hallway, the foursome tried to flush their nasal cavities with clean air. Theo dry-heaved again, placing his face between his knees. Madeleine stood over him, spraying herself, worried that the smell might have carried invisible organisms or spores that could burrow in her skin.

"I don't feel so good," Lulu mumbled. "Madeleine, will you spray some of that stuff on me? My clothes smell awful."

Madeleine stood over Theo and Lulu and sprayed them like a farmer dusting crops. Then, the girl turned with flushed cheeks to Garrison.

"Would you care for some?"

"Sure."

Madeleine savored the proximity to Garrison, standing closer to him than his own shadow.

"I think it works better if you stand farther back," Garrison said.

"Oh, yes. I was trying out a new method, but it appears less effective," Madeleine bumbled with embarrassment.

The door to the library creaked open and Mrs. Wellington exited with a cat under each arm.

"Are they okay?" Theo asked, upset at the sight of the animals.

"Of course; cats are carnivores. They love steak."

"Steak?" Lulu asked. "That was steak?"

"Oh, yes. Sirloin steak circa 1990."

"I'm sorry, but I don't understand. What is the purpose of a library dedicated to smelly food?" Madeleine asked.

"That may have caused permanent damage to my esophagus," Theo said seriously.

"Silly, silly boy," Mrs. Wellington laughed. "And to answer your question, the Library of Smelly Foods is used to keep Schmidty in line with the Casu Frazigu. Every time he complains, claiming he can't bear another bite of it, I bring him in here. After a few whiffs, his taste buds can't wait to get back to the Frazigu. Plus it is rather helpful when I get a contestant terrified of dairy products."

"I think I inhaled deadly spores from that steak. A vegetarian dying from steak — the cruel irony," Theo blubbered from the floor.

"Dear boy, you have such an exasperating temperament," she said with her lips darkening to an alarming shade of fuchsia, even for her.

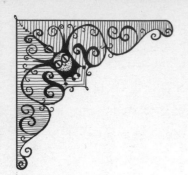

EVERYONE'S AFRAID OF SOMETHING:

Helminthophobia is the fear of

being infested with worms.

All you need is fresh air. To the polo fields," Mrs
Wellington said, leading the group down the
Great Hall.

Madeleine simply wasn't prepared to brave the polo
fields. With tears brimming in her eyes, she caught up
with Mrs. Wellington and grabbed the old woman's cold
hand. "Mrs. Wellington, please. I don't want to go outside. There are spiders, insects, and such," Madeleine
explained politely, albeit with a strained voice.

"Outside? Dear, don't be so narrow-minded. Not *all* polo fields are outside."

"Then how's the air going to be fresh?" Theo mumbled quietly to himself.

Mrs. Wellington proceeded down the hall with Lulu, Theo, and Madeleine trailing behind her.

Garrison, further behind everyone, scrutinized the doors along the way. He ran his fingers across a standard-sized wooden door, forgettable in every way except touch. Instead of sleek wood, Garrison felt the tight weave of a painter's canvas. It wasn't a door at all, but rather a painting of a door. The crevices and indentations of the wood were mere shades of paint tricking the eye.

"What's with the painting, Mrs. Wellington?"

The old woman stopped walking, as always in unison with the clock, some ten feet ahead of him. She turned and stared into his tan little face. The hall became uncomfortably quiet except for the clock and Madeleine's repellent spray.

"Did you think it was a real door?"

"Yeah."

"And it's really only a painting of a door. Contestant

Garrison, please tell me what you think that means in thirty seconds or less."

"That you ran out of doors?" Garrison said oafishly.

"You have much work to do on your elocution skills. All contestants should be prepared to answer questions intelligently in thirty seconds or less."

From behind Mrs. Wellington came Madeleine's proper British voice: "Mrs. Wellington? If I may, I believe the door represents that things aren't always as they seem. On occasion, it's necessary to inspect things, or people, a bit closer," she explained while staring directly at Garrison.

Mrs. Wellington nodded approvingly at Madeleine.

"I thought we were going to the polo field?" Lulu interrupted.

"A reminder to all, don't stand behind the horses; it's very dangerous," Theo said seriously. "My mom knows a woman who was kicked in the face by her horse. Her head swelled big as a basketball. After that she couldn't remember anyone's name, called everyone 'what's her name,' even herself."

"Yeah, right," Lulu said incredulously.

"It's true," Theo bellyached, "I met her at the Christmas party. She said 'hello, I'm what's her name. Pleasure

187

to meet you.' All because she walked behind a horse. If only I had been there to warn her," Theo finished spectacularly.

"Excuse me, Cowboy Chubs? Are you finished?" Mrs. Wellington asked exasperatedly while standing in front of the red and white gate.

The latch on the polo field gate was dated and rusty, seemingly from years of exposure. The lock squealed and grunted its way out of the corroded slot. Theo bit his lip, ruing the decision to remove the tetanus shot from his first-aid kit. The school nurse had claimed that rust didn't cause tetanus; a cut from rust merely created an ideal habitat for bacteria to breed. Of course, in the face of rust, Theo started to second-guess the nurse.

Unable to watch Mrs. Wellington jimmy the lock, Theo turned to the partial body of a 1959 DC-8 jet lodged in the wall opposite the polo field. The red, white, and blue United Airlines logo was faded from years of wear and tear in the air. Theo pushed his face against a small circular window, steaming it up with his breath. He spotted a snack cart, inciting a rabid desire for salted peanuts. Maybe Mrs. Wellington left treats in the cart to create an authentic experience. Theo imagined hiding out on the plane eating peanuts, missing his family, and sleeping. He would much prefer that to spending time with this group of risk takers.

Mrs. Wellington finally dislodged the rusted lock, opening the polo field's gate and releasing a wave of horse manure. Ripe and earthy, the scent prompted Madeleine, Lulu, Garrison, and Theo to wince.

"Wow, that is . . . ," Garrison mumbled.

"Nasty," Lulu finished his sentence.

"This is supposed to help us get over the steak?" Theo scoffed.

"Manure is a natural cleanser of the olfactory glands. Didn't you know that?"

"Nope," Lulu said glumly, revolted by the latest affront to her nose.

"That's why perfume counters often keep a small dish of manure for clients to sniff between scents."

"I've never seen that before," Madeleine said honestly.

"Don't feel bad; that's why you're here. To learn," Mrs. Wellington responded as she femininely sashayed onto the field.

It was approximately the size of half a football field with eight oddly tranquil horses standing in the center.

Murals of rolling hills and white clapboard fences surrounded the abnormally green lawn while sunlight poured through the plate-glass ceiling. Although seemingly pastoral, it was also curiously creepy. Madeleine remained close to the door. Having inspected the grass visually, she then did something extremely out of character. Madeleine touched the grass.

"Mrs. Wellington, is the grass artificial?"

"It's AstroTurf, dear. The next best thing to the real stuff."

"I'm afraid you're mistaken, Mrs. Wellington," Madeleine said assuredly, "it's far superior. Bugs can't live in plastic grass!"

"Are you starving these poor horses? No wonder they're so tired. Look at them, they're barely moving," Theo exclaimed.

"Barely moving?" Mrs. Wellington responded. "Theo, they're not moving at all. They're dead."

"Did you kill them?" Theo asked with his lower lip quivering.

"Kill them? Heavens no. I simply had them stuffed. Good job too — you can still ride them."

"Then how did they die?"

"A strange mold on their hay. It was devastating. I was heartbroken at the idea of life without them, so I built the polo field."

"This mold you mentioned, did you find the origin of it? Is it toxic to humans as well?"

"Theo, please don't concern yourself with that. To the best of my knowledge, Schmidty never cooks with hay," Mrs. Wellington said before pausing to glance at the ceiling, as if to think it over.

Meanwhile, Madeleine stopped spraying herself, instead focusing on the horses in the room.

"Not to be nosy, Mrs. Wellington, but were the horses' coats treated for insects and other organisms?" Madeleine asked.

"Of course!"

Relieved, Madeleine turned to explore her new surroundings. Mrs. Wellington then shook her head and mouthed "no" to the other students.

Lulu, Garrison, and Theo couldn't help but wonder what else she had fibbed about.

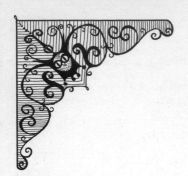

EVERYONE'S AFRAID OF SOMETHING:

Mastigophobia is the fear

of punishment.

The following morning Lulu, Madeleine, Theo, and Garrison cautiously settled into their silver desks and prepared for Mrs. Wellington's lesson. The night before the four children had discussed how they might escape from the school, but in the absence of any good ideas, they went to sleep, hoping the next day would bring better luck. The fact that the day was beginning in the classroom rather than the Fearnasium or any other crazy room in the house was a start.

"Contrary to the title, a beauty pageant isn't all about beauty. There are a great deal of other things that come into play — poise, personality, posture — just to name a few. And yes, I realize that none of you have the makings of pageant winners — well, except for Lulu," Mrs. Wellington said, "but there are still many important lessons that can be garnered from the art of pageantry."

"Mrs. Wellington, I can't speak for Theo, but I am a boy. We aren't into pageants. We don't wear lipstick, tutus, or crowns. Nothing pink," Garrison said harshly.

"I sometimes wear pink," Theo added before noticing Garrison's incredulous look, "but only around Easter."

"Trust me, Sporty, you of all people could use some pageantry in your life. And in case I hadn't made it clear, my lessons are not optional. I am like going to the dentist, school, or your grandparents' house — a necessary pain. So please close your mouth," Mrs. Wellington said with crimson-spotted lips. "Now then, let's begin with two of the most important skills: the smile and the wave. These will help you throughout life, serving you well at the mall, on a date, or just hailing a cab."

"I don't get it. What do smiling and waving have to do with fears?" Lulu asked.

"What a sharp cookie," Mrs. Wellington said, prompting Lulu to gloat at Theo, Garrison, and Madeleine with a smirk.

"The art of pageantry has absolutely nothing to do with fears. Not one little thing," Mrs. Wellington said. "Each of you has been given a pot of Vaseline."

"I'm terribly sorry to interrupt, Mrs. Wellington, but why we are learning pageant protocol at School of Fear?" Madeleine implored politely. "Wouldn't that be more appropriate for a beauty school or modeling school?"

"Honestly," Mrs. Wellington said before releasing a long and irritated sigh, "I haven't seen the likes of this since the Spanish Inquisition, which as you may recall started when Marcia de Sevilla tried to steal my crown at the Barcelona Hilton."

"Actually, I believe it was started by Ferdinand II of Aragon and Isabella I of Castile —" Madeleine stopped mid-sentence after noticing Mrs. Wellington's darkening lips. "Or on second thought, maybe it did start at the Hyatt."

"It started at *the Hilton*," Mrs. Wellington said with exasperation. "Contestants today have no regard for history. Haven't your parents taught you the importance of education?"

The odd old woman then adjusted her wig, took a deep breath, and applied more bubblegum lipstick. "Now then, please dip your index finger into the Vaseline and spread it slowly across your teeth," Mrs. Wellington instructed. "Any excess Vaseline may be wiped on the napkin or, if you're hungry, eaten. Unfortunately, Schmidty did not have time to flavor the Vaseline with Casu Frazigu, something about needing to sleep. Honestly, when men hit their eighties, it's one excuse after another."

Madeleine stared out the window, ignoring Mrs. Wellington altogether, which was no easy feat. Mrs. Wellington was at her most alert and insane when discussing the fine art of pageantry. Madeleine felt a terrible unease with the state of things. Not only was she separated from all the things she held dear in life — her family, bottomless supplies of repellent, her own personal exterminator — but she was learning absolutely nothing. When all was said and done, the girl would return to London just as hindered by insects as ever. The only difference would be a few pageant tricks up her sleeve.

"Oh Beekeeper? I need your attention in the front."

"My apologies, Mrs. Wellington," Madeleine responded while plastering her teeth with the thick opaque goop.

"And the veil needs to be raised."

"Is that absolutely necessary?"

"You can raise the veil or I will confiscate all your repellents, including the ones hidden in your luggage."

"But, how did you . . ."

"Schmidty may be blind, but he can still snoop with the best of them."

Madeleine acquiesced, raising the netted veil off her face.

"This stuff won't affect our teeth enamel, right?" Theo asked. "Because my dentist is really strict. I'm not even supposed to drink soda. He was a colonel in the army, so I don't want to make him mad."

"Theo, I am sure that someone somewhere cares to listen to you ramble on about your dentist, but it's not me," Mrs. Wellington said as she shoved a ruler in the back of his trousers. Theo's pants were already a little too snug for his liking. The addition of the ruler made them downright unbearable.

"Or me," Lulu added with a smirk as Theo feebly attempted to stretch the waist of his trousers.

Mrs. Wellington proceeded to place rulers in the back of Lulu's, Madeleine's, and Garrison's clothes, all of which had a great deal more give than Theo's slacks.

"One cannot wave properly without good posture. Your backs are to remain parallel to the rulers at all times," Mrs. Wellington said as she demonstrated the perfect posture, smile, and wave for the students to imitate.

"Fingers together, backs straight, smiles wide. Again! More Vaseline, Madeleine! Shoulders back, Theo! Fingers together! Backs straight! Smile wide! Garrison, that wave is entirely unacceptable! Do it again, Sporty!" Mrs. Wellington barked. "Again! Again! More Vaseline, Theo! I said more!" Mrs. Wellington's voice rose, channeling a dictator the likes of which the children had never seen.

By the time it was over, biceps and triceps stung from waving, cheekbones ached from grinning, and mouths bubbled with Vaseline. It was a strange brand of torture, but painful nonetheless. Even athletic Garrison felt the strain of these peculiar tasks. While his arms survived fine, his face was a mass of dull, throbbing pain.

The lesson was extraordinarily long, forcing the students to forgo lunch and rush to dinner without brushing their teeth or removing the rulers. Once seated stiffly at the dining room table, crows cawing in the background, the foursome wiped their well-greased mouths on Mrs. Wellington's pristine linen.

"You think this will stain the napkins?" Theo asked.

"Who cares about the napkins? We're stuck with a deranged beauty queen. I can't stop smiling, and I'm not even that nice," Lulu whispered.

"Finally, a little self-awareness," Theo said condescendingly.

"Shut it, chunky funk."

"Enough, Lulu," Madeleine butted in, "you're the last one who should be complaining; you're her favorite and the only one she deems pretty enough to win a pageant."

"You say that as if being teacher's pet to a waving weirdo is a good thing. Trust me, it's not. And if you're so interested in winning a beauty pageant, why don't you take off the veil?"

"Madeleine without her veil is like chocolate without peanut butter, salt without pepper, mayonnaise without mustard."

"Thank you, Theo. I am rather keen on the veil as

well," Madeleine said before sighing, "she simply doesn't know a thing about fears. I wouldn't be surprised if we went home worse off than when we arrived."

"Home," Theo stated dramatically. "Just hearing the word makes me miss my family. My family always fed me such delicious food. Have I mentioned that I'm really, really hungry? I need food that doesn't taste like maggot cheese. I need pasta. Or even just a slice of fresh sourdough bread with some butter, preferably salted butter."

"We have more pressing issues than getting you salted butter!" Lulu snapped.

"Someone needs a time-out," Theo whispered to himself before being interrupted by Garrison pounding his fists in frustration on the table.

"Why did I even come to this stupid place?" Garrison grunted angrily.

Naturally, at that very moment, Mrs. Wellington chose to make her grand entrance.

"Sporty, do you have Alzheimer's? Be such a shame, seeing as you're only thirteen. I suspect Schmidty has it, but alas, you can't ask him, since he's deaf. Perhaps you can write him a note about your condition after dinner," Mrs. Wellington said from the doorway to the Great

Hall. "Something short and pithy like, 'I can't remember, can you?'"

"Madame, it appears that it's you who can't remember. I am not deaf, but rather a tad blind," Schmidty calmly announced.

"Quite right. You are blind and a bit pudgy, in case you were interested," Mrs. Wellington responded.

"Mrs. Wellington, I'm pretty sure I don't have Alzheimer's," Garrison explained.

"Very well. But if you happen to remember that you've forgotten everything later on, let me know. In the meantime, let me remind you that you're here because you bluster and sweat in a very unattractive way at the sight or mere mention of water. If you like, I can do an impression?"

"No, thanks," Garrison said quickly as Mrs. Wellington, Schmidty, and Macaroni joined the children at the table.

The children may have remembered how they came to be at School of Fear, but now they were focused on how they could flee, as soon as possible.

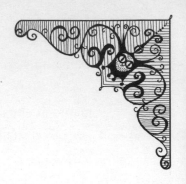

CHAPTER 18

EVERYONE'S AFRAID OF SOMETHING:

Eisoptrophobia is the fear of

mirrors or of seeing oneself in a mirror.

The following morning Garrison awoke with heart palpitations, covered in sweat. Next to him was a snoring pajama-clad bulldog; apparently Macaroni the dog had tired of sneaking into Theo's bed. Garrison stroked his soft head while racking his brain to remember what could have caused him to wake up with such anxiety.

Obviously, his first line of thinking focused around water. Had he dreamt of being lost at sea, trapped in the eye of a hurricane, or simply seated near a pool? Garrison wasn't sure exactly how to explain it, but this felt different. With Macaroni loyally at his feet, Garrison brushed his teeth, determined to let whatever he'd dreamed about go. He spat out the remaining bits of toothpaste and looked down at Macaroni. As Garrison peered into the brown sagging eyes of the semi-clothed dog, it came all at once.

Garrison had dreamt of the end of the summer, when he was to return to his parents in Miami. Garrison had told his father that he was still afraid of water. Mr. Feldman hadn't expounded on life's distaste of losers and babies; instead he had turned away from his son without a word. It was an epic failure, one too large for words to contain.

Garrison slipped downstairs, leaving his classmates happily unconscious in their beds. He didn't even know what he was looking for, but he wanted some kind of proof that this place would cure him. As he tiptoed down the Great Hall, his stomach began to churn with anxiety. He was at a circus, a veritable loony-bin. It was utterly inane to expect a woman with a home as eccentric as Mrs. Wellington's to actually be a true teacher.

While staring at the door to the Library of Smelly Foods, Garrison accepted defeat. He would return home just as big of a baby as he'd left.

Shortly thereafter, a depressed Garrison joined Madeleine, Theo, Lulu, Schmidty, and Macaroni for breakfast. The absurdity of the past few days had taken a toll on everyone, not just Garrison, leaving the group abnormally quiet. Forks scratched against china and Macaroni chewed loudly, but no one spoke. No one had even inquired where Mrs. Wellington was, and why she was late for breakfast. Of course, even if they had, no one would have guessed correctly.

"Ahhh!" Theo yelped as a large green swamp thing entered the dining room. It was the shape of a human covered head to toe in a soft green moss. Within seconds, the precise steps, inhumanely straight posture, and feminine mannerisms exposed the creature to be Mrs. Wellington.

"Oh stop, blathering boy, it's just Greenland fungus," Mrs. Wellington responded.

"Is that like gangrene?" Theo asked while pushing his chair away from Mrs. Wellington.

Before she could answer, Madeleine asked, "Do bugs live in that stuff?"

"Children, you act as if you've never seen someone dressed in fungus before."

"We haven't," Garrison responded.

"Well, I suppose if you don't spend much time in Northern Greenland, you wouldn't. Up there, you find entire towns dressed in fungus. They don't bother washing it off during winter. It's warmer than fleece, but much less expensive. The best part is that it's attracted to heat, so all a warm-blooded creature need do is touch it and — pronto — instant outfit."

"How do you take it off?" Theo asked.

"Follow me," Mrs. Wellington said as she began marching down the hall in sync, as usual, with the tick of the clock.

Halfway through the Great Hall, Mrs. Wellington stopped in front of a standard-sized patchwork gold door. The foursome squinted at the radiant door before Mrs. Wellington flipped it open, exposing wall-to-wall slimy green fungus. Somehow, the fungus was a bit more disgusting en masse than on Mrs. Wellington. Maybe she just wore it well; a stylish lady through and through. All the children knew for certain was that a room full of fungus made them queasy.

"Does it smell like mayonnaise, or am I imagining it?" Theo asked with a grimace.

"You are imagining it, Chubs; all I can smell are brussels sprouts," Lulu said.

"Contestants, the lot of you are ridiculous. It is all in your heads. The fungus is entirely odor-free. Here, take a sniff," Mrs. Wellington said as she presented her arm to the foursome, who unanimously declined the offer.

Madeleine still hadn't heard a definitive "no" regarding whether bugs inhabited the fungus and would not be going anywhere near the stuff until she knew for certain.

Mrs. Wellington stepped into the room of wall-to-wall fungus, immediately camouflaging herself.

"Watch closely," she instructed while hovering near the doorway, rattling a chain. As the children strained to focus on the blob, salt hailed down from the ceiling. Coarse and unusually heavy salt flakes washed over Mrs. Wellington, creating a large white dust cloud. Seconds passed and the haze cleared, showcasing a miraculously spotless Mrs. Wellington.

Mrs. Wellington stepped into the Great Hall and

closed the golden door. The foursome stood, mouths agape, inspecting her white nightgown for a speck of fungus, but there was none. It took a second for the children's eyes to make their way up Mrs. Wellington's body to her head.

When they did, the foursome screamed in unison as they stared into the face of death. Mrs. Wellington was a frightening sight without a drop of makeup, exposing grayish yellow skin splintered with bulging blue veins.

"Contestants, I am terribly sorry. I've let you down as a beauty queen. Today I am not prepared. Your queen has faltered. Your icon has cracked. Please understand, it was your unbridled curiosity for the Greenland fungus that overwhelmed me, prompting me to momentarily lose sight of my role as a beauty queen. Can you ever forgive me?"

"Um, well, that depends," Lulu said haughtily. "Are you going to make us do more pageantry exercises?"

"Of course, whatever you wish," Mrs. Wellington said, completely misreading the situation.

"Um, we most definitely do not want to do any pageantry today," Lulu said assertively. "We're talking no Vaseline."

"In that case, no pageantry. Contestants, you have my word. Consider it scrawled in lipstick. Absolutely no pageantry or Vaseline today. How about ten minutes of imaginary exercises in the Fearnasium, so Schmidty has time to apply my makeup and hair?"

"Schmidty does your makeup?" Lulu asked.

"Actually, that makes a lot of sense," Theo said while reflecting on Mrs. Wellington's sometimes questionable makeup choices. "Yup, it's all coming together for me."

As soon as their ashen-faced, bald-headed headmistress exited the Great Hall, Garrison started toward the Fearnasium."

"Um, you're welcome," Lulu said sarcastically to the group. "A little appreciation would be nice."

"Thank you, Lulu, it's much appreciated," Madeleine said with lackluster. "Now we ought to get started in the Fearnasium."

"Or we could just imagine we were imagining our activities in the Fearnasium?"

"Now we're talking," Garrison said while cracking a smile.

"You are absolutely devilish, Lulu," Theo said with great admiration.

"I know," she said pridefully. "What would you guys do without me?"

"I'd probably have higher self-esteem and I suppose Madeleine would be less insecure about not being spotlighted for pageants, and Garrison . . ."

"Theo, it was a rhetorical question. Even I know that," Garrison said as he walked toward the classroom.

"The rhetorical question," Theo rued to himself, "gets me every time."

Theo fell in line behind Garrison as the foursome made their way to the classroom.

The classroom was nearly dark with the thick velvet curtains drawn, blocking all the day's light. It reminded Madeleine of the ride to School of Fear, where vines and trees all but deleted the sun from view. Thankfully, cracks of light managed to break through between the dense curtains and the windows. Lulu glanced at the slivers of light as Mrs. Wellington prepared the slide projector for the day's lesson. The projector's humming was jarringly loud to the foursome. Of course, they were accustomed to teachers using nearly silent laptops for presentations.

Garrison sat with impeccable posture, a side effect of Mrs. Wellington's beauty pageant education. Not that he even realized it; Garrison was far too preoccupied hoping that the day's lesson would finally focus on fears. It didn't have to be the key to the Magic Kingdom, instantly eradicating his fear, but just some good sage advice. Garrison needed something to take home to his father.

Behind Garrison, Theo sat, also with perfect posture, rubbing his tongue around his mouth, desperate to eradicate the leftover slime from yesterday's lesson. While admittedly, his gums did feel softer, he wasn't used to his mouth having the consistency of a slip-and-slide. Next to Theo, Madeleine performed her usual dusting of repellent with near-perfect posture. In front of Madeleine, Lulu defiantly hunched her shoulders, a testament to her pride in escaping Pag Ed.

"Contestants, when I went upstairs, Schmidty screamed. He was that taken aback that I had allowed you, my disciples, to see me in the light of day without a shred of makeup or hair. As you know, my platform has always been that 'a beauty queen is always prepared,' and for floundering this one time, I apologize," Mrs. Wellington said with misty eyes. "Now then, as you requested, we are skipping pageantry today and will instead focus on something a bit more traditional — history."

"History? You're going to teach us history? What about something to do with fears?" Garrison moaned, "since this is the School of *Fear* and all?"

"Sporty, history is the second most important subject a boy can study. You shouldn't scoff at that."

"Let me guess, pageantry is the first," Garrison said with bubbling agitation.

"Exactly! Who said you weren't sharp?" Mrs. Wellington responded. "Was that Lulu? Or Madeleine?"

"It wasn't me," Madeleine quickly interjected.

"What am I supposed to tell my dad? He expects me to come home cured!" Garrison exploded. "Do you know what that means? It means afternoons at the beach! Surfing lessons! Pools! Whitewater rafting! I feel sick even saying the words! How am I going to face my dad?"

"You tell your bossy, old, grouchy father that getting over your fears is a process, one we must confront daily, and that if he has a problem with that, he should investigate why he is more afraid of your fear than you are," Mrs. Wellington said with the confidence and clarity of a bona fide certified teacher.

Garrison, shocked into silence, stared at Mrs. Wellington, whose lipstick Schmidty had accidentally applied slightly outside her lips. It was a spectacularly astonishing moment: Mrs. Wellington had actually taught him something. Beyond the wig, bad makeup, and total insanity, there appeared to be a sliver of knowledge regarding fears.

"Thank you," Garrison mumbled, incapable of articulating anything more. He still wasn't any closer to being cured, but he felt a great deal lighter.

"You're welcome, Sporty," Mrs. Wellington said kindly. "It seems like just yesterday, my own mother was teaching me the Bill of Rights," she said while dabbing her eyes. "When I learned that the Bill of Rights secured my right to bear charm, freedom to bleach, and protection from unreasonable tweezing and plucking, well, history just came alive. I suddenly understood how important it was, and today I hope I can help you see that as well," Mrs. Wellington said while clicking the first slide.

A black-and-white photo of an elaborately dressed baby in a bassinet filled the screen.

"It all started at Murphy General Hospital," Mrs. Wellington said while gazing at the baby.

"Stunning, isn't she? In fact, Edith was so gorgeous the doctor asked to purchase her. Of course, her parents declined, although they certainly were flattered."

"Wait, a doctor tried to buy a baby?" Lulu asked incredulously.

"As you can see, Edith was an exceptional beauty; no one could blame the doctor for momentarily losing his bearings."

"Now then, first grade," Mrs. Wellington said while clicking the projector. "Edith was very smart; a true hit with the teachers. Sometimes, they even brought *her* apples. That's how much they liked her."

"Who is Edith?" Theo asked genuinely. "The governor of Massachusetts? State senator?"

"Dear boy, I haven't aged that much, have I?"

"Wait, the history lesson is about *you*?" Theo responded.

In that moment, Garrison was more perplexed than he had ever been. How is it possible that the same woman who just handed him fantastically smart advice was now conducting a history lesson on her own life? Not to mention doing it in the third person.

Mrs. Wellington clicked the next slide and a young caramel-haired boy, no more than ten, filled the screen. His face was angelic, a true beauty. Though the boy was only onscreen for a second, Garrison was instantly confounded by his familiarity.

"Uh! What is that doing in here?" Mrs. Wellington grumbled to herself.

"Who was that?" Garrison called out as Mrs. Wellington quickly snapped to the next slide of herself.

"Who?"

"The boy."

"What boy? Oh, that boy," Mrs. Wellington said with sudden recognition. "His name is Theo. Honestly, I thought you would have learned each other's names by now."

"Not Theo," Garrison responded, "the boy in the slide. Who is he?"

"O-oh," Mrs. Wellington stammered, "He came with the projector. Moving on."

"No, I've seen him before. I'm sure of it."

"Oh Garrison, no one is really sure of anything in this crazy beauty pageant of life. Now moving on . . ."

"No, I know I've seen him before. He's the missing kid from the poster by the B&B," Garrison said, suddenly sure of himself.

"Is that poster back up?" Mrs. Wellington said with bloodred lips. "I'm going to have some serious words with Schmidty."

The foursome stared at Mrs. Wellington as her face twisted with fury. Minutes passed before her cheeks returned to their normal contour and her lips arrived at a more natural shade. Sensing the eye of the storm had passed, Garrison pressed on.

"Who is that boy?"

"Again with this? His name is Theo."

"The boy in the slide!" Garrison retorted with intensifying annoyance.

Mrs. Wellington sighed, adjusted her wig, and dabbed her upper lip before speaking.

"Perhaps he was once a student here."

"What's his name?"

"I can't be expected to remember every student's name. Why, there are days I can hardly remember

Schmidty's name. Just last week I called him Harriet! And to make matters worse, he responded. He too thought his name was Harriet! Do you see how confusing it all is? It's simply impossible for me to know who that boy is!" Mrs. Wellington exploded harshly.

"Got it," Garrison said, surprised by her intensity and anger. "Never mind, then."

"On to my cotillion," Mrs. Wellington hollered before pausing to collect herself. "Edith always had such a lovely little cherub face," she continued while gazing at the slide of herself in a white gown and elaborate jewelry.

"Do most American girls wear diamond tiaras and necklaces to their cotillions?" Madeleine asked sincerely.

"Diamonds are such a headache. Why, just looking at this photo makes me want to reach for an Excedrin. They are the worst. The absolute worst. Whoever said diamonds are a girl's best friend never owned any. All diamonds ever got me was a bunch of dead guys. Four to be exact."

"Did you say dead guys?" Theo asked.

"Yes, I said *dead* guys: the Malicious Melvin Brothers' Circus. Those scoundrels trained in rock climbing for a year before they burgled me."

"And you killed them?" Theo asked with surprise.

"Why is it that you are always asking me if I killed someone? Do I look like a murderer? Do I dress like a murderer? What exactly about my beauty says murderer? Had you said ballet dancer, model, actress, I would understand, but murderer? Would a murderer have perfectly painted pale pink fingernails?" Mrs. Wellington asked while displaying her immaculately manicured nails.

"Sorry, it's just where my mind goes," Theo said with a shrug. "You absolutely do not look like a murderer. I'm sure that if I had seen you back in the day when you still had your own hair, I would have totally thought you were a model."

"Thank you, Theo," Mrs. Wellington said with a nod before returning to the story at hand. "Not only did I *not* kill those circus creeps, but after they grabbed my diamonds, I offered them pocket money and a snack for the return journey. Unfortunately, my calm attitude spooked them, and they became frantic and cut through the forest instead of following the road back."

"And?" Lulu asked.

"And nothing. Schmidty found my tiara and necklace four years later atop a stack of old bones. Apparently the men had starved to death, or been eaten, or, well, anything. Schmidty isn't much for forensics. What can I tell you? The forest, like a casino, always wins. That's why you should never gamble, or enter the forest. And above all, never underestimate Schmidty," Mrs. Wellington said seriously. "Class dismissed."

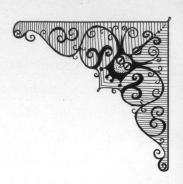

CHAPTER 19

EVERYONE'S AFRAID OF SOMETHING:

Arachibutyrophobia is fear of
peanut butter sticking to the roof of the mouth.

Abernathy

Macaroni loved his food — that much was obvious. The dog regularly sprayed the table with spots of drool while enthusiastically crunching through piles of kibble. So when he lifted his head and ignored his half-full bowl, the lunch crowd took note.

With their eyes dutifully on Macaroni, Mrs. Wellington, Schmidty, and the students wondered what epiphany could possibly have distracted him from his beloved kibble. It was oddly disconcerting to watch Macaroni freeze under the weight of his canine instincts; after all, this was a dog who willingly wore pajamas to bed. Macaroni's growl was low and fierce, immediately dissolving all lighthearted explanations for his behavior.

"Why is Macaroni growling?" Madeleine, who was seated closest to the dog, asked.

"I'm not sure," Mrs. Wellington responded while staring at Schmidty.

"You don't think he sees a spider or something?" Madeleine continued.

"No, Madeleine, I assure you he doesn't growl in response to spiders," Mrs. Wellington said curtly.

Madeleine instantly began dreaming of a spider and insect seeing-eye dog. She would cherish such a companion, lavishing him or her with filet mignon, rack of lamb, and other delicacies. Madeleine's daydream was cut short when Macaroni once again increased the decibel of his growl.

"Perhaps Mac has something stuck in his throat," Schmidty said.

"Should I give him the Heimlich?" Theo offered while jumping to his feet.

"No," Mrs. Wellington said dismissively. "If he had something in his throat he'd cough. This is a growl."

"Madame, I'm not sure dogs know how to cough. Perhaps this is as close as he can get."

"That is absolutely ludicrous. If a dog can sneeze — and I've heard him sneeze — then he can cough."

"If you say so, Madame."

Just as Schmidty finished speaking, the plates, candelabras, and glasses on the table began to rattle.

"I thought you said there weren't earthquakes in Massachusetts!" Theo hollered at Mrs. Wellington.

The rattle morphed into a thud, a loud and repetitive pounding noise from beneath the table.

Mrs. Wellington turned paler than usual; why, even her lips were blanching. Schmidty held tight to his comb-over as his face twisted with uncertainty.

"It couldn't be . . . ," Mrs. Wellington muttered in shock.

"It's the big one," Theo warbled hysterically, "drop and cover," he added as he dove beneath the table.

"Madame, you promised me that you would warn me before he came!" Schmidty screamed at Mrs. Wellington.

"I'm sorry, Schmidty, honestly, I am. But I didn't

know. This must be an emergency. There is no other reason he'd use the chute!"

"Yes, Madame, perhaps you're right. This could be an emergency. Perhaps the wretched beast wagered his children on one of his 'sure things' and lost!"

"That only happened once, twice at most. And may I remind you, he didn't use the chute on either of those occasions! This must be something . . . terrible!" Mrs. Wellington snapped to Schmidty.

"It's a sad day when losing one's children at the track doesn't constitute terrible!"

"Oh, stop that! This is hardly the time for moral superiority!"

"Tell my family I loved them," Theo called out from beneath the table.

"Theo," Madeleine said sweetly as she leaned over his quivering body, "it's not an earthquake."

"How do you know?"

"Well, earthquakes aren't localized to such small areas. If this were an actual quake the entire room would be affected, not just the table."

As Madeleine finished explaining the situation to

Theo, the pounding became more intense. Between thuds, a muffled voice hollered and groaned.

"Schmidty, he's climbed hundreds of feet up a rope ladder! This is an emergency!"

"Up, children! Up!" Schmidty roared at the foursome in a decidedly un-Schmidty-like tone of voice. "Mr. Garrison, grab the left side of the table."

Garrison, surprised by Schmidty's take-charge manner, decided it best not to question the order.

The two pushed the table and all of its contents to the left side of the dining room. Lulu and Madeleine stood near the door to the hall, with Theo cowering awkwardly behind them. He still wasn't absolutely sure that this wasn't some strange earthquake mutation and thought it wise to stand in the door frame, on the off chance the rumbling spread.

Schmidty hurriedly threw the green shag carpet to the side, igniting a dust storm years in the making. When the layer of filth cleared, Mrs. Wellington, Schmidty, the students, and Macaroni stared intently at a trapdoor. Scrawled in messy red lettering was a note, "For Dire Disasters Only." It was only the sound of yet more banging and muffled screaming that pushed Schmidty to actually unlock and open the trap door.

A large swatch of tangled and unnaturally dyed brown hair came into view first. Even from a few feet away one could tell that the hair was thick and coarse, much like the bristles of an old broom. Beneath the wildly unkempt brown mess were a full two inches of white roots. As odd looking as it was to see a man desperately in need of a touch-up, it was nothing compared to what came next.

The face was gruesome, very much in line with a dermatological science experiment gone awry. The man's pale skin was knotted into knobs of flesh that dotted his face like bushels on a field. Long white hairs sprung from the protrusions, some hanging long and straight while others curled tightly. In great contrast to his pale skin and wild white facial hair was the yellow of his eyes and teeth. So small and yellow were his teeth that on the rare occasion he tried to smile, they recalled corn on the cob. Of course, he didn't actually smile; he only frowned less.

Theo screeched at the sight of the man before turning away.

"How ghastly," Madeleine inadvertently muttered aloud before quickly covering her mouth in shame.

Before them was a sweaty, out-of-breath monster of a man, hanging perilously from a rope ladder in a dark chute.

"Munchauser," Schmidty announced with disdain as he stared mercilessly at the repugnant man.

"Who'd you think it was?" Munchauser said in a gravelly voice that sounded like the last stages of laryngitis. "Wait, don't tell me. I'll bet you one hundred dollars I can guess who you thought it was."

"You vile . . ." Schmidty started to react venomously, only to be interrupted by a frantic Mrs. Wellington.

"Oh stop it," Mrs. Wellington snapped, "Schmidty, help him!"

"I'm sorry, Madame, but this man . . ." Schmidty trailed off as he begrudgingly pulled Munchauser from the chute.

It was only when the abnormally tall man stood fully erect before the foursome that they were able to garner the full grotesqueness of Munchauser's appearance. At six feet he was tall, but his thin and lanky limbs created the illusion that he was much closer to seven feet. Dressed in a hand-tailored garish purple suit, with racing forms protruding from his breast pocket, Munchauser was striking, but not in a good way.

With ragged and dirty fingernails, Munchauser brusquely pushed Schmidty out of the way, determined to be as close to Mrs. Wellington as possible.

"Welly, I've missed you," Munchauser said to Mrs. Wellington before turning to the students nearby. "I see you have germs here as usual."

"Munchauser! What are you doing here?" Mrs. Wellington interrupted harshly.

"Welly, we have a problem," Munchauser announced in his crackly voice.

"Well of course we do! You just used the Dire Disaster Door. However, I still don't know what the problem is!"

"You want to guess? I'll give you twenty dollars if you get it right, but if you don't you owe me your sapphire ring."

"Munchauser! Would you stop with the bets! What is happening?"

"Welly, it's a serious situation. I've got a lot to tell you," Munchauser said while approaching Lulu. "Five bucks says I can guess your name."

"I don't have five dollars," Lulu responded calmly.

"What? Your parents didn't give you any spending cash?" Munchauser asked with frustration. "Fine, what do you have on you? Fifty cents? Seventy-five? Come on, I'll work with you."

"Munchauser!" Mrs. Wellington screamed.

"What? It's just a little friendly wager."

"Why did you just climb two hundred feet up a dark hole? Is there or is there not an emergency?"

"And bankruptcy doesn't count," Schmidty said snidely.

"Why don't you pull your pants a little higher, old man?"

"Munchauser, for Heaven's sake, what is happening?"

"Welly, before I tell you, do you even want to try to guess? It could be easy money on your part. Of course, should you win, I'll have to write you an IOU 'cause I left my checkbook in the bunker. But you know I'm good for it."

"Tell me this instant or I will cut you out of my will!"

"Abernathy is back," Munchauser spit out instantaneously.

229

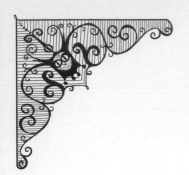

CHAPTER 20

EVERYONE'S AFRAID OF SOMETHING:

Atychiphobia is the fear of

failure.

Shrill, hysterical, and bananas were the only words to describe Mrs. Wellington after the news came. Utterly incapable of conversing or standing still, Mrs. Wellington stormed through the house saying the name Abernathy over and over again. She would start low, almost at a whisper, and build up until she was screaming at a piercing level. All the while, she clacked through the Great Hall, passing through the airplane, around the jumbled mess of stairs, across the polo field, through the Fearnasium, upstairs, back downstairs, into the kitchen, the dining room, the classroom, and so on. Behind the frazzled and frantic woman were the arguing men, Schmidty and Munchauser, each elbowing the other to get closer to Mrs. Wellington.

"Welly! What were you going to guess? Please tell me. I need to know. Do you want me to guess what you were going to guess?"

"Madame, please stop! All this storming around can't be good for your knees or my arthritis!"

However, Mrs. Wellington paid them no mind and continued storming hysterically through the house.

Trailing vigilantly behind Schmidty and Munchauser were Madeleine, Theo, Garrison, Lulu, and Macaroni. It was an odd sort of parade.

"What is going on?" Garrison screamed at no one in particular.

"Personally, I'm relieved. I prefer her lawyer to an earthquake, even with all the bets," Theo said in an oddly calm voice.

"Hello? Schmidty? We're talking to you!" Lulu hollered.

"This is absolute mayhem! Bedlam! Pandemonium!" Madeleine said to Theo. "What is happening here? I never thought it possible, but this school has actually become crazier than before!"

"Did you see his fingernails?" Theo responded, totally ignoring Madeleine's comments. "A year's worth of bacteria under there. There is no way I'm shaking his hand or touching anything he touches. That kind of dirt, well, it can put you in the hospital for weeks. I honestly wouldn't be surprised if there were rare viruses under there. On second thought, an earthquake would have been safer."

"Theo, did you even hear a word I said?" Madeleine retorted.

"Madeleine, we are in the presence of a Center for Disease Control offender, someone who balks at basic hygiene. I don't have time to keep track of every little thing you say!"

And with that the frenzied parade meandered through the house, the participants muttering to themselves.

One by one, people peeled off. First was Lulu, who decided she would rather do just about anything other than follow a bunch of lunatics around the manse, especially since everyone was ignoring her questions. The next defector was Theo, who took Macaroni with him, as the dog had begun panting rather loudly. In truth, Theo had been winded as well; neither dog nor boy was prepared for such a workout. Theo and Macaroni ducked into the kitchen, where they scoured cupboards and drawers for the best of the Casu Frazigu–free food. Theo also took it upon himself to close the Dire Disaster Door, after worrying that one of his classmates or even Macaroni might fall in.

Madeleine departed the tour when it ventured outdoors. She had no intention of entering the spider and bug kingdom. Moreover, this reminded her that Munchauser had climbed through a dark cavern, where heaven knows what may have attached to the putrid man. Sickened by the thought, she knew it was time to wash her hair with the hard stuff: boric acid shampoo.

Garrison stayed the longest, mostly out of curiosity.

He simply had no idea what was happening or how it would turn out.

"Welly, you were just joking when you said you'd cut me out of the will, right?"

"I'm not ready for Abernathy!" Mrs. Wellington cried.

"Would you stop about the will!" Schmidty roared at Munchauser.

"Bet you a hundred dollars I'm getting more than you, fat fool."

"You don't even have one dollar, let alone one hundred, you ugly beast!"

"Take that back or I'll sue you for slander!"

"Abernathy!" Mrs. Wellington continued.

"Please, Madame, please, calm down."

By this point Garrison had completely stopped asking who Abernathy was, because, quite frankly, he realized no one had any intention of telling him. So instead of questioning, he simply listened and lent a hand to Schmidty when the old man began hobbling. This was more exercise than Schmidty had done in twenty years, as evidenced by his messy façade. Schmidty's slacks had fallen below his massive gut; his white dress shirt was partially unbuttoned and covered in perspiration circles; but worst of all, his hair had fallen. The elaborate comb-over turban was in the process of unfolding, and it wasn't pretty.

By the tenth lap around the classroom, Schmidty heeded Garrison's advice and agreed to sit down.

"Madame needs me. . . ."

"Schmidty, you can barely walk, and your hair, well, it's not good. You need to rest."

"Well, maybe for a minute. Madame can handle Munchauser alone for a bit, I suppose."

"Schmidty, I've just spent the last few hours chasing you around the house. You need to tell me who this Abernathy guy is."

"Dear Mr. Garrison, it's a rather depressing story. I'm not sure I'll be able to tell it without a few tears."

"Okay," Garrison said uncomfortably, confused why a grown man needed to cry while telling a story. On second thought, Garrison wasn't sure he could handle seeing Schmidty cry, especially with his hair in such ruins. The man looked downright wretched, and he hadn't even started crying yet. "Maybe you should try and keep it together, you know, in case Mrs. Wellington needs something."

"You are quite right, Mr. Garrison."

"Okay, now out with it. Who is Abernathy?"

"I have long tried to get Madame to accept the Abernathy situation, but she wouldn't have any of it. If I'm being brutally honest, Madame isn't terribly good at admitting her shortcomings. She prefers to feign ignorance of any inadequacies. Why, she often pretended she had forgotten who the boy was, which I clearly knew to be false. Occasionally she would even mumble his name in her sleep, sometimes apologizing, other times angry —"

"Please, Schmidty, I'm really trying to be patient, but who is Abernathy?" Garrison interrupted with mounting frustration at Schmidty's verbose tale.

"He is her greatest weakness, and as any good fortune cookie can tell you, we are only as strong as our weakest part."

"Please Schmidty, for the last time, who is he?"

"Her one failure . . ."

"What does that mean? Tell me who he is in plain thirteen-year-old English."

"Abernathy is the one student she couldn't help throughout the years. So many have come and gone, I've lost track. All have gone on to lovely lives, except for Abernathy. She never could help him, and oddly the more she tried, the worse he became."

"Schmidty, are you really telling me that Mrs. Wellington, the crazy lady in the wig who has been teaching me how to wave with Vaseline all over my mouth, has actually helped people with their *fears*?" Garrison said with profound shock.

"Oh, yes. Madame is a brilliant teacher."

"And when you say 'students' you mean actual human beings, not the cats?"

"Oh, no. I am referring to children, human children. Madame has treated so many; you should see the load of holiday cards she receives every year."

"I don't even know what to say."

"The failure of Abernathy has tortured her, almost destroyed her many times. And when I say failure I mean catastrophic, dismal, utterly horrendous, tortuous failure."

Garrison sat shell-shocked, unsure what to think

of the information he had just been given. Something wasn't right. Maybe Schmidty was older and a bit more senile than he seemed. Garrison stared as the old man attempted to reposition his comb-over without the aid of a comb. It was no simple task, as the man usually spent twenty minutes with a vat of hairspray to get it in place. Just as Garrison was preparing to bring Madeleine down to redo Schmidty's hair, a roar cut through the house. This wasn't a roar like that of a lion; it was a great deal closer to that of a diesel engine, only categorically human.

The disturbing roar roused the curiosity of all who heard it. Madeleine, dressed in her pink dressing gown with a built-in veil, immediately ran downstairs, worried that Munchauser and Schmidty had finally come to blows. In defense of Schmidty, Madeleine was prepared to unleash a hailstorm of repellent. In the kitchen, Theo and Macaroni both froze mid-chew. Normally, Theo would have bolted immediately, but he simply didn't think he could handle any more drama, so he continued eating, albeit with an ear out for other suspicious sounds. While Theo wasn't absolutely certain, he thought Macaroni was chewing lighter in an effort to help them monitor what was happening in the house. Just as Theo shoved an exceptionally large piece of bread into his mouth, he heard Schmidty's sweet voice crack in agony. Macaroni took off first, with Theo fast behind him.

Theo's mouth became dry with fear as he followed Macaroni toward the polo field. The bread in his mouth was dense and now seemingly impossible to swallow. Without doubling back to the kitchen for a glass of milk, Theo had no other choice but to spit the large and half-chewed wad of bread on the floor before entering the field.

Madeleine, Munchauser, and Schmidty were standing in a line, staring ominously at the floor while Lulu and Garrison stood off in a corner whispering.

"What's all the ruckus?" Theo said as he pushed his face between Schmidty and Munchauser to see what was happening. It was a sight Theo would always remember. More disconcerting than anything he had ever experienced before, even his grandmother's passing. There in front of him was Mrs. Wellington's ashen face and pale blue lips. Her eyes were closed and her wig was crooked, partially exposing her scaly bald head.

"Welly's dead," Munchauser announced coldly.

CHAPTER 21

EVERYONE'S AFRAID OF SOMETHING:

Mnemophobia is the fear of

memories.

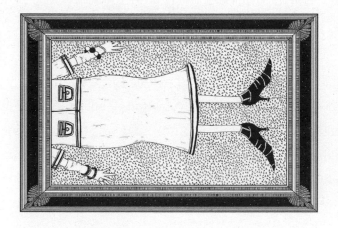

Theo couldn't speak. No words could express the finality he was battling. It was all-encompassing and brain jumbling. His teacher — whom he had never really liked in the first place — was dead. And she would never again be alive. Mrs. Wellington would never know who the next president would be, what movies would capture the country's heart, or what advancements would be made in the science of hair rejuvenation. When these events happened, Theo would remember that Mrs. Wellington, odd as she had been, was not around to share in the experience. Then a visual of her lifeless corpse would flash through his brain.

Theo didn't remember how he got from the polo field to his bed, but he did. All he knew was that when he woke up, both Macaroni and Madeleine were lying sullen-faced next to him. Lulu was curled up in a tight ball on the floor of the boys' room with one hand over her left eye. Theo wasn't sure where Garrison was, and he was far too stunned to use his vocal cords yet.

As Theo ran through yet more changes the world would encounter without Mrs. Wellington, he began to think of all he had lost. Theo would never know her favorite book, her best friend, or the name of Mrs. Wellington's mother. Did she have any children? Grandchildren? Great-grandchildren? Great-great-grandchildren? How had she come to run, albeit ineptly, this school on the hill? Sure, he could ask Schmidty, but it wouldn't be the same. He wouldn't hear it from Mrs. Wellington. Sad and stunned into silence, Theo felt ill at ease over everything except his desire to go home.

Garrison chose to stay with Schmidty as he lovingly painted Mrs. Wellington's fingernails, applied makeup, and brushed her wig. He just didn't feel right leaving the old man alone with Munchauser. Mrs. Wellington's dead body didn't freak Garrison out as much as the strange smirk on Munchauser's face did.

"I bet you ten bucks she prefers red for her funeral," Munchauser said as Schmidty applied a thick layer of pink lipstick.

"I hardly think this is the time for bets," Schmidty seethed, "not to mention, how would we settle a bet about what she prefers when she's dead . . . ," he choked out.

"I didn't think about that," Munchauser said while pacing in front of the dead body. "Of course, we will be able to settle another bet."

"Don't you even care that Madame is dead? She's gone! Left us forever!"

"Of course I care, old man. But I'm a businessman, and as such I must put my feelings on the back burner until everything is settled, which includes the reading of the will and our friendly wager about who she leaves more to."

"I never took that bet, you creep."

"Well, you didn't specifically not take it, so it counts in my book. Now Welly left her last will and testament in the safe, so let's wrap this up and get down to business."

"When you say *this* do you mean Madame? Do you expect me to wrap her in newspaper and toss her out with the old flowers?" Schmidty roared.

"No, of course not. We'll leave her on the field until you can dig a grave. And don't worry, I'll turn up the AC."

Garrison watched the two men, both buzzing with emotions, and wondered where this situation left him and the others.

"Here's a blanket," Munchauser said as he grabbed a pink cashmere throw from a bin on the side of the field. "Cover her up, and let's get down to it."

"Your compassion is overwhelming," Schmidty fumed as he covered up his Madame.

Schmidty then laid his head across Mrs. Wellington's chest and closed his eyes. His left hand fumbled
until it found one of Mrs. Wellington's hands and
squeezed it tightly. Even with his eyes closed the
emotion was so unbearably raw that Garrison
looked away.

"I shall be with you again soon, Madame," Schmidty
said in a soft, almost childlike voice.

The sentiment of Schmidty's goodbye irritated
Munchauser, as if it was interrupting his plans.

"Will you save it for the funeral? I've got a lot
to do around here. You have no idea the kinds of
plans I have for this place," Munchauser said,
almost salivating at the notion of taking over the
estate.

"You are as dense as you are deranged. Madame may
have left you some cash to see a dermatologist and a la-
ser hair removal specialist, but trust me, Summerstone
and all that's in it will be left to me. She knew that I
would protect her legacy."

Schmidty turned away from Munchauser, clearly
tired of arguing.

"Mr. Garrison, are the others all right?" Schmidty asked Garrison.

"They're okay. Not Theo, but I don't think any of us expected him to take this well."

"Is he crying?"

"No, he's still silent. To be honest it's a little creepy, like he's in a coma with his eyes open or something."

"Mr. Theo always was such a sensitive soul, he just needs time to mourn — we all do. . . ."

"Hey, kid?" Munchauser called out to Garrison.

"Well, not all of us, just those of us with feelings," Schmidty corrected.

"I said 'hey kid,' why didn't you answer? You think you're too good to answer me?" Munchauser asked Garrison angrily.

"Sorry," Garrison mumbled.

"You better be, because I don't know if you heard but I'm in charge now."

"Stop that," Schmidty interrupted.

Completely ignoring Schmidty, Munchauser continued speaking to Garrison: "Assemble your comrades in the drawing room in five minutes. As your new head-master, I want you all there for the reading of the will, the passing of the torch," Munchauser said with his version of a grin, which clearly displayed his pronounced gums. If Munchauser *did* inherit the school, Garrison definitely hoped he would use some of the money to sort out his teeth.

"I suppose the sooner we get this over with, the sooner you'll leave," Schmidty hissed to Munchauser.

"Or the sooner *you'll* leave. I will take such pleasure in throwing you and that fat dog off the mountain. The realization of a lifelong dream."

A bit later, Garrison guided Madeleine, Theo, Macaroni, and Lulu down the Great Hall and into the classroom. Schmidty had lit several candles and arranged numerous vases of pink roses throughout the room. On the coffee table, surrounded by tea candles, were a couple of small black-and-white photos of Mrs. Wellington as a child. Schmidty and Munchauser were standing directly in front of the coffee table, each with a hand on a large and exquisitely wrapped pink envelope.

"I'll read it," Munchauser said.

"I don't trust you," Schmidty said spitefully.

"Well I don't like y—"

"Give it to me," Garrison interrupted, desperate to get the reading of the will over with as soon as possible.

"Fine," Munchauser acquiesced after Schmidty nodded in agreement.

"However, before you read the will, I would like to make a small speech. I think it's going to be hard to talk over your sobbing later," Munchauser said pointedly to Schmidty.

Lulu and Madeleine bookended Theo and Macaroni on one couch while Schmidty and Garrison sat on the other. Munchauser, seemingly energized by Mrs. Wellington's death, paced in front of the somber group as he prepared to speak.

"As some of you may know, I am Welly's lifelong attorney, the most trusted member of her inner circle, a true friend," Munchauser said while poorly pretending to be overcome by emotion. He went for his handkerchief in his breast pocket but instead pulled out a betting form, then another and another. Soon the floor was littered in forms, and Munchauser decided it easier to simply skip the theatrics.

"As it takes a while to liquidate assets, not to mention that I have no interest in refunding any of your parents' money, I will be finishing the summer as your headmaster. And please feel free to call me master, for short," Munchauser said with another one of his attempts at a smile. "I will teach you the fine art of life at the track, including debt collection and placing bets. The house takes all winnings, and you're responsible for your losses."

"Excuse me, sir, my name is Madeleine Masterson, and I would like to make another suggestion. Perhaps we could simply be lowered off the mountain and returned to our families."

"Yeah, we don't want a refund," Lulu added. "We'll even pay you more to let us go —"

"Children, trust me, this won't be an issue once the will is read. Garrison, if you wouldn't mind starting," Schmidty interrupted.

Both Munchauser and Schmidty watched Garrison

with the utmost confidence as he quickly unwrapped the intricately tied pink envelope and pulled out a single sheet of paper. The handwritten will was hardly a surprise, as Mrs. Wellington was hesitant of technology such as computers.

"'I, Edith Wellington, of enviable style and overwhelming charisma, do hereby declare this to be my last will and testament expressly revoking all wills and codicils heretofore made by me. To the Impoverished Pageant Scholarship Fund, I bequeath all my wigs, dentures, girdles, false eyelashes, acrylic nails, makeup, crowns, sashes, and vats of Vaseline. To both the Bald Brothers Institute and the Comb-Over Collective, I bequeath five hundred thousand dollars in the name of *my late* best friend, Schmidty. No other man so dedicatedly displayed the dangers of male hair loss. To my attorney, Leonard Munchauser, I bequeath the amount of one dollar, which, as you may recall, you bet me at our first meeting, absolutely sure that you would die first. Well, you were wrong. And may I add that had you been right, I would have no one to pay, since you would be dead. All remaining cash and assets, including Summerstone, stocks, bonds, and CDs, I bequeath to my beloved dog, Macaroni.'"

CHAPTER 22

EVERYONE'S AFRAID OF SOMETHING:

Somniphobia is the fear of

sleep.

Garrison and the others had fallen asleep long before dinner, utterly drained from the horrors of the day. The arrival of Munchauser, the Abernathy parade, Mrs. Wellington's death, and finally the reading of the will were more than most could handle in a year, let alone a day. By 11:00 PM, both Munchauser and Schmidty had retired for the night, leaving Summerstone in sheer darkness.

Having always been a light sleeper, Garrison immediately woke when he felt a tickle on his forearm. Without opening his eyes, he swatted what he presumed to be a fly and tried to fall back to sleep. Seconds later, he felt the same soft tickle on his arm, prompting him to sit up in bed.

"Mr. Garrison," a weak voice whispered.

"Schmidty?"

"Shhh . . . we must keep our voices down."

"What are you doing on the floor?" Garrison asked, peering over the edge of his bed. Lying flat on his back, clad in striped pajamas and a sleeping cap, was Schmidty. And if that wasn't strange enough, he was carrying a long feather duster in his hand. Garrison smiled kindly at the old man.

"Maybe I should wake Madeleine or Theo," Garrison offered, believing that either one of them would be better equipped to handle Schmidty's grief.

"No. No. I must speak with you. You're the only one I trust to handle this."

"Okay," Garrison relented. "Back when my Uncle Spencer died, I thought I'd never get over it, but with time . . ." Garrison trailed off, struggling to find the right words to reassure Schmidty.

"Mr. Garrison, please. We don't have time for psycho-analysis. I've just spent the last twenty-five minutes pulling my body down the hall like a very bloated snake."

"What? Why?"

"It's the only way I could be sure not to bump into something and wake Munchauser. I can barely see in the daytime, let alone at night."

"What's going on?"

"Munchauser is up to something. He dismantled the crane after you kids went to bed. I saw him through the telescope; he threw the hook off the mountain. He doesn't know I saw anything because when he returned to the house, I pretended I had been grooming Madame the whole time."

"That's a lot of makeup, even for Mrs. Wellington."

"Mr. Garrison!" Schmidty huffed.

"Sorry."

"When Munchauser returned he spent the rest of the night examining the will. Reading it over and over again."

"I wouldn't worry, Schmidty; unless he can morph into Mac, there isn't a whole lot he can do."

"No, Mr. Garrison, you're wrong. When an animal inherits money, there always has to be a guardian. Someone put in charge of the animal and the trust."

"Oh, well, that's obviously going to be you."

"No, the will didn't stipulate who the guardian was; all Munchauser has to do is take Mac. Don't you see, he'll get everything? Summerstone and Mac are all I have left. I can't let him take them. Please, I need your help."

"Schmidty, he's more than twice my size. I don't think I can take him."

"Dear Mr. Garrison, not that! I need you to help me get Mac out of here. At first light, I want you and the others to bring Mac to the dining room. I'm going to smuggle you out of the Dire Disaster Door. It will drop you in Munchauser's bunker at the base of the mountain. Then all you have to do is follow the road into town."

"Are you going to come with us?"

"No, I need to act like everything is normal, distract

Munchauser for as long as possible so he doesn't know you've gone."

"What about Abernathy?"

"He won't leave the forest, and Mr. Garrison, under no circumstances are you to enter the forest."

"That won't be a problem."

"Good. Now you'll need some things for the journey, just as a precaution, should you run into any problems along the way. Take this list," Schmidty said as he passed a folded white note to Garrison.

"I can't read it in the dark."

"Don't worry, once you get to the Great Hall, you'll be able to light a candle without Munchauser seeing."

"Okay, I'll get the others."

"No, wait. Give me thirty minutes to pull myself back to my room so I'll be able to intercept him in case he gets out of bed."

"He's in Mrs. Wellington's room?"

"Yes, he said he wanted to be reminded of her essence, but I'm quite sure he's in there pilfering odds and ends to pawn."

"Schmidty, I have a question. And I need you to

think very hard before you answer. Is there any water —"
Garrison stopped mid-sentence, ashamed that he was
thinking of himself at a time like this.

"No. The road stays clear of the river. You'll be fine.
I'm sorry to have to ask you to do this, but I have no
choice."

"Don't worry, Schmidty, we won't let anything happen to you or Mac."

Schmidty quietly rolled onto his stomach and began
pulling his rotund body toward the door. Perhaps it was
Garrison's nerves or his fatigue, but he had never known
time to move so excruciatingly slowly. Unable to wait,
Garrison attempted to read the list but couldn't make
out more than a few letters. He glanced at the clock; it
had only been three minutes.

Garrison concentrated on Theo's and Macaroni's
breathing, counting the seconds between each inhalation. The two had unconsciously synchronized their
breaths while lying side by side. He worried how Theo
would absorb the news of Macaroni's precarious status,
let alone the journey into town. Rather intelligently,
Garrison decided to wait until after he had the girls in

tow to wake Theo, who hadn't spoken since Mrs. Wellington's unfortunate passing.

Just when Garrison thought he could wait no more, the clock struck midnight. He released an irritated sigh and threw back the bedspread. The fear of knocking into something and waking Munchauser made Garrison second-guess every shadow. It took him nearly five times as long as it normally would to pass through the bathroom and enter the girls' room. Luckily, the return trip with the girls was much faster, having already completed the course once.

Standing around the bed, the three of them watched Theo and Macaroni exhale at precisely the same moment.

"Lulu, cover Theo's mouth in case he screams. Maddie, I think he'd take the news best from you."

"All right," Madeleine acquiesced, "I suppose that's true."

"Are we really going to do all this for a dog?" Lulu asked.

"Yes," Garrison huffed before turning to Madeleine. "You need to lift the veil. Sometimes it can freak people out when they're not expecting it." Garrison thought back to the first time he saw Madeleine on the bus from Pittsfield.

Lulu hated the feel of Theo's warm breath on her hand, but she agreed that there was a good chance of him screaming, especially after the day he'd had.

"Um, what are you waiting for? He's drooling all over my hand," Lulu barked at Madeleine, who quickly shook Theo's arm while gently saying his name.

"Theo, Theo, Theo. Wake up. Theo."

Theo's eyes nearly bulged out of his head when he saw the three of them gathered around his bed. However, impressively, he didn't try to scream. Once that was established, Lulu removed her hand and wiped it aggressively against Theo's comforter.

After learning that Macaroni and Schmidty were in danger, Theo instantaneously rose to the occasion. Well, technically he asked to go home first, but after being denied by Garrison, he happily rose to the occasion. Theo agreed to join them on the mission downstairs. Apparently, the idea of Munchauser destroying Mrs. Wellington's legacy by selling off Summerstone and evicting Schmidty was enough to get Theo fully talking again. He even offered to carry Macaroni down the stairs, but rescinded the offer after attempting to lift the fifty-plus-pound dog.

"We're in this together. Right?" Garrison whispered to the group as they prepared to exit the boys' bedroom. "No one falls behind."

Unaccustomed to this sort of pep talk, the three responded to Garrison's encouragement with weak nods.

Garrison, Lulu, Madeleine, Macaroni, and Theo tiptoed out of the boys' room at exactly seven past midnight. Garrison led the pack down the shadowy hall to the top of the stairs. Unfortunately, as the group descended, the wooden planks creaked loudly under their feet and paws. The house was so incredibly silent that it was hard to gauge just how loud the stairs were and if they could actually wake Munchauser.

Nervous about letting Schmidty down, Garrison paused to think before deciding to walk as close to the wall as possible. The floorboards still moaned, but much less. After a few steps, Garrison heard a scratching sound, followed by a waft of sulfur and a flash of light.

"What are you doing?" Garrison whispered angrily to Madeleine.

"It's a bug-repelling candle. Spiders love the dark, plus it will help us see."

"What if Munchauser gets up and sees the candle-light?" Garrison stuttered.

"It's better than one of us falling. Munchauser will definitely get up then," Madeleine responded firmly. "Or worse, if a spider lands on me, I'll scream bloody murder."

"I don't even like candles, but I think Madeleine's right, we need the light," Theo said diplomatically.

"Fine," Garrison relented.

"Seriously, if someone gives me a candle as a gift, I always send a note thanking them for putting *a lethal weapon* into my sweet, innocent young hands. I consider it a public service."

"Theo, I'm glad that you're speaking again, but this is *really* not the time," Lulu said with irritation. "And who in the world is giving you candles?"

The group tiptoed through the pink foyer, past the

multitude of pageant pictures, to the start of the Great Hall. The tick-tock of the clock echoed loudly in the children's ears as they read Schmidty's list.

Garrison —

The following things are needed to get you safely into town. I've left a satchel in the kitchen to pack these items for the journey.

SNACKS — In order to get Theo and Mac to town they will need sustenance. Neither one of them are at their most cooperative when they haven't eaten.

MADAME'S POTENT SMELLY STONES — To be used in case of an emergency. These can immobilize a person for at least two minutes.

GREENLAND FUNGUS — A fast and thorough disguise that will help you blend into any green background.

MACARONI'S SHOES — he has a strange aversion to the sensation of cobblestone on his paws. His favorite yellow booties are in the back of the utensil drawer in the kitchen.

*Be brave. Words cannot describe my gratitude
to the four of you.*
Schmidty

While Garrison surveyed the list with the girls, Theo
rubbed his temples to release the tension. Standing directly atop the loudly ticking clock in the floor, Theo
began to pace anxiously. The clock was the first door in
the Great Hall and one of the few located in the floor
rather than the walls. As Theo trod gently over the
clock, his right foot hit the clock's metal edge, cracking
it open ever so slightly. Theo used his foot to further
open the clock door. Silver wheels, pins, bolts, and coils
shimmered in the candlelight.

Lulu, Madeleine, and Garrison joined Theo to inspect the hatch when an excruciating pain pierced their
eardrums. It was the loudest sound they had ever en-
countered, pure auditory torture. The children grabbed
their ears as Macaroni howled in agony. Dogs have
vastly superior hearing to humans, thus making Macaroni's pain all the more intense.

The auditory feedback echoed through the hall,
bouncing from door to wall to window and back. Theo

buzzed with reverberations as he threw his body against the clock door. Maybe it was the lasting effect of the clamor, but it wasn't until Madeleine, Lulu, and Garrison pushed against Theo that he could close the door.

Similar to the effects of a stun gun, the sound left the children and Macaroni completely still. Ringing swished from their brains to their inner ears to their middle ears and finally their outer ears. It was a massively debilitating experience for all involved. Theo, for instance, would normally bawl at being trapped beneath three bodies. However, the sound left him so dazed, he merely shut his eyes. Lulu, who lay on top of Madeleine, pushed Garrison off her before wobbling to her feet for exactly one point five seconds. She then collapsed in a pile next to the others.

Garrison carefully avoided Lulu's body when he attempted to stand and regain his bearings. After years of playing sports, he was accustomed to being tackled, though nothing could compare to the throbbing in his temples. As the blood began to drain from Garrison's head, a frightening thought suddenly dawned on him: Munchauser must have heard the noise.

"Get up! Get up! We have to get upstairs!"

From beneath Madeleine's veil, Garrison saw a green complexion. She was clearly on the precipice of a barf attack. Garrison pulled Madeleine off Theo while trying to ignore the intense pounding in his head.

"That's what they should have used on Manuel Antonio Noriega Moreno," Madeleine babbled incoherently to Garrison.

"Maddie's delirious," Garrison said to the others.

"No, I'm not," Madeleine said defiantly, or as defiantly as she could without vomiting. "He was a Panamanian dictator; the U.S. blasted rock music to get him to leave the Apostolic Nunciature, where he was hiding out."

"How on Earth do you know this?" Lulu asked from the floor.

"I read a lot. Don't feel bad, it's terribly hard for my peers to keep up."

"The ringing, the ringing. Will it ever stop?" Theo asked, removing his hands from his ears.

"It's already been a minute or so. Why isn't Munchauser down here?" Madeleine asked reasonably.

"There's no way he didn't hear that," Lulu retorted, "even if he sleeps with earplugs."

"My ears are still ringing. Do you think this is permanent?" Theo moaned. "I'll be deaf within the hour. I'm the new Helen Keller."

"Except you can see *and* hear!" Lulu angrily exploded.

"Not for long."

"You are *such* an overreactor," Lulu said with an eye roll.

"Enough!" Garrison insisted. "We don't have time for this. Madeleine and I are going to take Mac to pack food and get his shoes. Can I trust you two to grab the smelly stones and fungus?"

"I wouldn't trust me," Theo said honestly. "Maybe to conduct a safety lesson, but even that I could mess up."

"We'll be fine," Lulu said confidently as she pulled Theo toward the library.

The Library of Smelly Foods was easy to navigate, as the jar they went in search of sat alone on the bronze shelf. Theo, against his better judgment, agreed to climb the ladder attached to the wall to claim the stones. He pushed himself along the wall, getting closer and closer to the little jar, approximately three times the size of a thimble. Of course, every few seconds, Theo felt it necessary to pause and shoot terrified looks to Lulu.

"Would you stop that? You're *not* going to fall."

"How do you know? I must be at least fifty feet off the ground. I could easily slip and die."

"Try ten feet, and if you're so afraid of heights, here's an idea: stop looking down!"

"Don't yell at me. This is very stressful. I'm like an air traffic controller up here!"

"Theo, I've barely slept; are you sure you want to test my patience today?"

"Way to offer sympathy, Lulu."

Now in arm's reach of the miniature jar, Theo closed his eyes and leaned to the right. After feeling around for a few seconds, Theo's chubby fingers stumbled upon the glass jar. He quickly leaned back, adjusted his grip on the ladder, and opened his eyes. The small, irregularly shaped yellow stones were crammed tightly in the jar.

"Don't drop the jar; Mrs. Wellington said the stones are the smelliest things in the entire library."

"Would you tell an air traffic controller not to screw up because the fate of millions was in his hands? No, because you wouldn't want to make him more nervous than he already was, especially if his palms sweat when he's nervous."

"So let me get this straight, you're the air traffic controller with sweaty palms?" Lulu huffed in frustration.

Theo groaned with annoyance while descending the ladder with one hand.

"I am serious, Theo, you cannot drop that!" Lulu screeched. "I almost died when she opened that steak. Just thinking about it makes me sick!"

"Lulu Punchalower, will you shut your trap? You are distracting me, and I am already a highly distractible person, in case you haven't noticed," Theo yelled back as he took another step down the ladder.

Lulu pursed her lips and remained quiet as Theo wobbled and groaned his way to the last step. Once back on the ground, Theo smiled, mission accomplished. Approximately half a second after Theo smiled, the jar slipped through his soft, stumpy fingers. Lulu's face contorted in terror as she fell to her knees, plugging her nose in preparation.

Theo opened his mouth to scream "no" but found that nothing came out. As is often depicted in films, time slowed as Theo flung his body against the floor. He extended his arm as far as possible, literally stretching his muscles to the max. A mere inch from the ground, he managed to slide his cupped alabaster hand underneath the jar. It was a heroic moment, or so Theo thought, as he lay on the floor, staring at the small and potentially dangerous jar.

"What are *tonsil* stones?" Theo asked as he read the small label on the lid.

"What?"

"It says *tonsil* stones, like the things in our throats."

"I'm gonna barf. That is so nasty. It's old food that gets stuck in your tonsils and rots."

"Maybe you should hold them?" Theo motioned with the jar.

"No way."

"Fine," Theo relented. "What's next?"

"Greenland fungus."

Theo visibly cringed. Something about the soft, slimy surface made his stomach flip even more than the tonsil stones.

"Don't worry, I wouldn't think of giving you any more responsibility."

"Finally, someone who understands me."

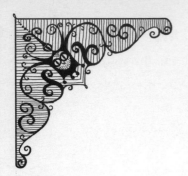

CHAPTER 23

EVERYONE'S AFRAID OF SOMETHING:

Autophobia is the fear of

being alone.

After passing a few hours in bed, sunrise finally arrived and with it the day's daunting mission. Lulu and Madeleine groggily entered the bathroom, prepared to make their way to the boys' room, then downstairs. Lulu, a ball of tension at the prospect of entering a hole in the ground, coughed loudly as Madeleine doused herself with repellent.

"Will you knock it off?" Lulu quipped.

"Excuse me, Lulu, but we are about to traipse through the homes of spiders, crickets, centipedes, millipedes, cockroaches, and much more. I am more than justified in performing a thorough spray-down."

Lulu touched Madeleine's shirt, then immediately wiped her hand on her jeans.

"You're soaking wet." Lulu stopped to sniff Madeleine. "And you stink. What is that?"

"Basil and eucalyptus oils; they're natural bug repellents. You certainly don't expect me to brave the outdoors without extra protection. I mean honestly, Lulu, it is hardly appropriate for you to fault me for defending myself," Madeleine said sternly, or as sternly as Madeleine knew how.

"It seems like overkill, but whatever."

"Lulu, you are the most insensitive girl in the universe! Do you have any idea what I am going through?" Madeleine shot back.

"You? What about me? I have to crawl through an underground tunnel."

"So do I!"

"Yeah, but you're not afraid of them!"

"Yes, I see your point," Madeleine said rationally.

At that exact moment, Garrison threw open the bathroom door, bleary-eyed from lack of sleep.

"Do you have Mac?"

"What? No, he's with Theo," Lulu said.

"No!" Garrison screamed as the reality dawned on him.

The foursome bolted down the stairs to the dining room, where they found Schmidty standing next to the Dire Disaster Door.

"He's gone!" Garrison announced.

"What?" Schmidty asked with terror creeping into his voice.

"Munchauser stole Mac!"

"No wonder the chute was already open. I thought you kids did it last night in preparation," Schmidty said as he fell to his knees.

"I'm sorry, Schmidty," Theo warbled. "I don't know how I didn't wake up! This is all my fault!"

"No, no, it's not. I just can't believe I've lost Madame, Mac, and now my home."

"No! We're not letting that happen," Garrison said defiantly. "Maddie, hand me the satchel. We're going to get Mac back."

"The satchel's gone," Madeleine said sadly. "Munchauser must have taken it."

"Forget the bag," Garrison ranted as he lit the candelabra and walked toward the tunnel. "Are you ready?"

Madeleine nodded, then quickly sprayed herself once over in repellent. Theo ran to the kitchen, only to return seconds later with fistfuls of chocolate.

"Theo, are you sure it's a good idea to eat so much chocolate?" Madeleine asked kindly, worried he might become ill on the journey down.

"I want to eat as much as humanly possible . . . in case I . . . d-don't ever . . . get to . . . eat chocolate . . . again," Theo stuttered between bites.

Garrison lowered himself first into the tunnel, precariously holding the candelabra as he descended the rope ladder. Next up was Madeleine, who silently prayed for a spider- and insect-free journey before following Garrison into the tunnel. Theo shoved the last of the chocolate into his mouth and hugged Schmidty with his chocolate-stained hands.

"Tell my family I loved them and make sure my mom doesn't feel guilty about the cell phone thing if I die. I'm sure there's no service up here anyway," Theo said with tears in his eyes.

"Mr. Theo, I can't thank you enough. Be brave; I know you will see your family soon."

Lulu, who had been unusually quiet, stood frozen next to Schmidty. While her body remained eerily still, her left eye twitched rapidly.

"Come on, Lulu," Theo called from the tunnel.

"I can't . . . I can't . . . you'll have to go without me. . . . I can't go . . . in there. . . ."

"Ms. Lulu, you must go. They need you. I don't think they'll be able to do it without you."

Lulu's breaths were short and stilted as she held her left eye, now pounding painfully.

"I can't breathe and I'm not even in there yet. I'm sorry, but I can't do it. I'm staying here with you, Schmidty."

"Lulu Punchalower," Theo hollered, "I need you! Who will be mean to me? Who will keep me in check if you're not here? I'm liable to have a bout of hysterical blindness if you're not with me to tell me to shut it!"

"Chubs, I'm sorry," Lulu said with deep disdain for herself.

"But Lulu, we're like the Three Musketeers, plus one. It won't be right unless you come."

"I . . . I . . . can't. . . ."

"Ms. Lulu, I understand. It's all right. Who knows, maybe it's better if you stay with me."

"Thank you, Schmidty."

"I know Madame would have understood if she were here. She probably would have eased you into the idea one rung at a time," Schmidty said thoughtfully before turning directly to Lulu. "Perhaps, in her memory, you could just go down to the first rung, then come out. I know it would have made her so proud."

"I don't know, Schmidty."

"Um, hello? We're waiting in here!" Theo yelled out.

"Please, Mr. Theo. Give us a second," Schmidty said into the tunnel before turning to Lulu. "It would mean so much to me."

Lulu couldn't say no to Schmidty's desperate and de-pressed face, so she took a deep breath and climbed into the hole.

"You came?" Theo said jubilantly upon sight of Lulu.

"Don't get your hopes up; I'm not staying."

"Actually, I'm afraid you are," Schmidty said as he deftly sliced the rope ladder in one fluid move.

"No, Schmidty!" Lulu screamed as her freckled face burned bright with fright.

"I'm sorry, but they need you!" Schmidty called out as the foursome disappeared into the black abyss.

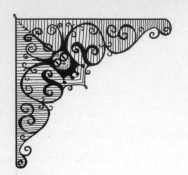

CHAPTER 24

EVERYONE'S AFRAID OF SOMETHING:

Chirophobia is the fear of

hands.

Black. It was completely black. The candelabra had been extinguished as the group fell down the steep tunnel. By the time they tumbled onto a level surface, Lulu's terror was increasing at an exponential rate. Her neck grew rigid from escalating panic and her breaths morphed into a labored wheeze. This was the situation she had lived in fear of her whole life. It was a place without light, without a foreseeable exit, and with the dwindling of the others' voices, she was virtually alone.

Lulu curled up into a ball and closed her eyes. Of course, there was no difference between having her eyes shut or open, since it was pitch black. She fought desperately for a gulp of air, suddenly realizing there was a limited amount of oxygen underground. Lulu thought of her parents, brother, teachers, and friends. They all seemed foreign, almost imaginary.

Prepared to face the terrifying reality, Lulu finally opened her eyes. Lifting her head was a great deal harder than she expected, which she could only assume was the result of her near suffocation. Where was Theo when she was ready for *her* moment of melodrama?

Lulu crawled aimlessly through the tunnel until happening upon a narrow divide of dirt. To the right she felt a tunnel, and to the left another tunnel. She debated which one could possibly lead her out of this nightmare. Perhaps both led to a dead end; there was simply no way of knowing.

Lulu moved to the right, for absolutely no reason other than needing a resolution. She crawled as fast as humanly possible considering her constricted lungs, throbbing head, and the detonation of her worst fear.

All Lulu wanted was to not be there, in the overpowering darkness.

"Please, please, please," Lulu mumbled, pleading with herself to continue. Somehow she summoned enough courage to propel herself through the tunnel, only stopping when her hair caught on something. Reaching up, Lulu discovered small twigs jutting out from the dirt.

At that very moment, Lulu decided she wasn't going to go without fighting for her friends — and Schmidty and Mac, too. Lulu's small and nimble hands grabbed what she realized were tree roots and pulled. She yanked and dug with the ferocity of a gopher. As Lulu frantically dug, she heard a voice. Was she imagining it? It was more than possible considering the destruction her mind had undergone since entering the black hole.

"Mom . . . Mom . . . Dad! If you can hear me? I'm stuck!"

A moment of hope passed through Lulu's body. But Was it really him? Or was this a figment of her imagination?

"Do you think the leaves are poisonous?" Theo's voice echoed.

"God save our gracious Queen, Long live our noble Queen."

"Why are you singing about saving the queen?" Garrison asked with irritation. "She's not trapped! She's sitting pretty in her castle!"

"Sorry, it's England's national anthem; I thought it might bring us a bit of luck."

"Luck? I think what we need is a gardener and our mean friend Lulu!" Theo hollered.

"Just be happy your head's not stuck in these things. Somehow I doubt you'd look good bald," Garrison responded.

It wasn't Lulu's imagination; she had found them! Well, not exactly, but they were close. Oddly, her focus on reaching them eradicated the ache behind her left eye and her asthmatic breathing as she slogged through the mud, listening, while the voices grew louder.

"Is that a spider?" Madeleine asked frantically.

"Where?" Garrison asked.

"That black ball. There. Oh no, I can't move!"

"Maddie, please stay calm. I don't even think it's alive. It's a part of a leaf or something."

"What have we done to deserve this?" Theo whined. "Why us? I've always been nice to people, and I assume Madeleine has too. Garrison, well, he's come around, and isn't that what matters?"

Lulu continued down the tunnel, yelling, "I'm coming!"

"Lulu?" Theo screamed back.

"Yes, it's me!"

"Lulu! Thank Heavens!" Madeleine yelled.

Lulu popped her muddy face into the light, immediately squinting as her eyes burned. It was the most fabulous burning sensation she had ever known. Never in her wildest dreams did she think she could be this happy to wander, covered in mud, into a greedy lawyer's underground office, and find her friends trapped.

Lulu took in the dark and dingy room, walls plastered with old betting sheets and racing stories from the newspaper. In the center of the room was a large metal desk covered in chipped black paint. It was quite a change from the pageant photos that decked the walls of Mrs. Wellington's mansion.

To the left of the large metal desk, Theo, Madeleine,

and Garrison were entangled, much like flies in a spider's web, in a network of vines set up to catch all that exited the main tunnel. Lulu had climbed out of a tunnel at least ten feet away, completely avoiding the sticky mess.

"Forget the queen! God save Lulu!" Madeleine exclaimed with tears in her eyes. "Do you see that black thing to your left?"

"Maddie! There is no time for small bits of lint. We need help! Schmidty is depending on us to get Mac back," Garrison said severely.

"Schmidty, if you can hear us, we won't let you down! We won't let you lose Mac or the mansion," Theo announced with flair.

"Ten minutes ago I would have made fun of your drama school performance, but I can't now. I'm too happy to see you," Lulu said sincerely.

"Oh no, we're running out of oxygen," Theo said, half-serious. "Lulu's hallucinating. She thinks she likes me."

"Lulu, how about some help? It's trickier than it looks. Munchauser set up these vines to trap us," Garrison said. "There's a letter opener on the table, but you need to be extra careful not to touch any of the vines or we'll *all* be stuck here," Garrison instructed tensely.

Without further delay, Lulu grabbed the letter opener off the desk and dragged a wooden crate over to Garrison.

"Be careful, Lulu."

"Stop talking. You're distracting me, Garrison."

"Don't distract her," Theo interjected.

Lulu's small and dirty right hand shook while navigating the overlapping vines.

"Lulu, you've got to calm down."

"Um, hello? Obviously, I don't *want* my hands to be shaking. I can't stop them!"

"Wait. Stop for a second and think of something comforting," Garrison responded.

Lulu rolled her eyes.

"Like a cell phone," Theo replied.

"Or bug repellent," Madeleine added.

Lulu sighed and then thought for a second about how happy she had been to hear her friends' voices from inside the tunnel. The tremors halted and her mud-stained hand moved with the precision of a surgeon. Garrison wanted to tell Lulu to hurry up, but decided he couldn't take the chance of rattling her newfound confidence. Lulu sliced the vines near his hands, dropping him to freedom, and then happily passed Garrison the letter opener so that he could free Madeleine and Theo from the web.

Madeleine immediately sprayed herself from head to toe. Seconds later, she turned the repellent to a worthy adversary, the small black thing she'd spotted from the web.

"It's a piece of dried-up old wood. What a relief!" Madeleine exclaimed. "That was a close call."

"Team, we need to focus. Why would Munchauser build an office underground?" Garrison asked as he peered around the dust-filled room.

"It's an old fallout shelter," Madeleine said as if it were the most obvious of answers.

"A what?" Lulu responded.

"A bomb shelter. They were predominantly built in the nineteen-fifties during the Cold War, in case of a nuclear attack."

"Well, how are we supposed to get out of here?" Lulu said as she began to sense a low rumble of claustrophobia.

"There's the door," Garrison said, pointing ahead a few feet.

Mere nanoseconds after Garrison opened the door he slammed it shut.

"Are we sure there isn't another way out?" Garrison asked with sweat pooling on his upper lip.

"Other than crawling up a two-hundred-foot tunnel?" Theo asked sarcastically.

Garrison's face was pale and sweaty from the stress of what he had seen, but he wiped his brow and once again grabbed the copper knob. He entered the room, followed by Lulu, Madeleine, and Theo.

The instantaneous screaming was louder than any child had ever produced in the history of children. It lasted less than eight seconds, but left an intense, unforgettable ringing in the ears.

CHAPTER 25

EVERYONE'S AFRAID OF SOMETHING:

Geliophobia is the fear of

laughter.

Five exposed bulbs burned brightly on the ceiling of the bunker, illuminating every nook and cranny. In the center of the room was a mass of old rusty cabinets stacked high with betting forms, books, and papers. In the corner there was a ladder mounted on the wall that led to a submarine hatch on the ceiling.

Clearly, it wasn't the desk, papers, or books that set the children off, but something far more sinister. Mounted on a copper plate behind the cabinets was a recognizable face, a friend. His sagging brown eyes and exaggerated underbite were unmistakable. Macaroni.

"Mac," Garrison muttered, defeated.

"Macaroni. How could he?" Theo said as he began to weep.

"I don't understand. This doesn't make any sense. He needs Mac to get the money," Lulu said logically.

"And how'd he stuff and mount him so quickly?" Garrison asked suspiciously as he approached the wall.

"A reputable taxidermist takes nine to twelve months, not nine to twelve minutes," Madeleine added. "Not to mention, where's the body?"

"It's not Macaroni," Garrison said from below the taxidermy head. "It's Cheese."

"What is Cheese doing in here?" Theo squawked.

"He's dead," Lulu added sarcastically. "That's his stuffed head on the wall."

"Do you think Munchauser killed him?" Theo asked with fear brimming over in his eyes.

"Maybe he just likes the way stuffed heads look on the wall. My granny has a couple of deer heads at her country home. I've always found them rather distasteful, but to each their own," Madeleine explained.

"We don't have time to stand around here and figure out why Munchauser has a stuffed dog head on the wall. We need to get Mac back," Garrison said powerfully, "before he ends up looking like that."

After unscrewing the submarine hatch, Garrison led the others out of Munchauser's dungeon. The hatch was wedged between the start of the gray cobblestone road and the granite mountain, which housed Summerstone. Just as the children remembered from their trip with the sheriff, vines grew from one side of the forest to the other, encapsulating the road in foliage. Without the security of traveling in a vehicle, the forest's dark and dense overgrowth appeared particularly sinister.

"The sooner we start, the sooner we'll get out of here," Lulu said, starting down the road. "And I don't know about you, but this place creeps me out."

"As long as we stay on the road, we'll be fine," Garrison reminded the group.

"I'm walking in the middle. I don't want to get too close to the forest," Theo said before lowering his voice, "because you know who lives in there."

"Schmidty said Abernathy won't bother us as long as we stay out of the forest and I'm not going in there," Garrison said while surpassing Lulu and taking the lead.

"Do you hear that?" Madeleine said frantically while drenching herself in repellent. "Insects! Bugs! They're talking to each other, preparing to swarm!"

"I don't hear anything," Lulu said. "Maybe chattering from the squirrels, but that's it."

"A swarm is coming! Do you hear me, people? A plague!" Madeleine screamed.

"A plague?" Theo asked. "Nothing good is ever attached to a plague. There's never a happiness plague or a safety plague. Always bad stuff. Anyone remember the bubonic plague?"

"Madeleine," Garrison said firmly, "You need to get ahold of yourself. There is no swarm, no plague, nothing."

"But that sound!" Madeleine railed on hysterically. "Don't you hear it? Surely, you must. It's getting louder by the second!"

"There is no sound!" Garrison said harshly. "It's in your head. You need to get a grip before you give Theo and yourself a heart attack!"

"They're coming," Madeleine said with tears in her eyes. "I can hear them buzzing toward me, preparing to attack at any second."

"Guys," Theo said to Garrison and Lulu. "She looks pretty certain. Maybe we should listen to her. Maybe a plague really is coming and she's more tuned in from all her years of avoiding the outdoors. She's like a super-hero with an extra sense, a bug sense. Do you understand what I am saying?"

"No," Lulu said definitively, "I absolutely do not understand what you are saying or thinking or . . ."

"They're here!" Madeleine hollered, immediately breaking into a frenetic, awkward run that included shaking her arms and legs while coating her body with repellent.

While Theo hadn't seen who "they" were, his instincts told him to run, so that's exactly what he did.

"You have got to be kidding me? Fireflies? That's the plague that's coming?" Lulu said while stifling her laughter. "You would have thought insects had bred with spiders the way she was screaming."

"Don't joke about spidsects!" Madeleine shouted at Lulu. "It's blasphemous!"

"In fairness to Maddie," Garrison said, feeling particularly guilty for having been so dismissive earlier, "I've never seen fireflies travel in such a tight pack before. I guess it could be kind of freaky if you're not prepared for it."

"I think they're pretty, kind of like a comet," Theo said while watching a small pack disappear back into the forest.

"Pretty? Ha! Do they have antennae? Multiple legs? Sticky feet? Hairy bodies?" Madeleine asked pointedly.

"Don't worry," Theo said calmly, "It's not like they can sneak up on you. They have lights on their backs."

"I suppose that's true," Madeleine acquiesced while looking cautiously around her, "but I still wouldn't call them pretty."

The cobblestone road twisted tightly with hairpin curves, obstructing the group's ability to see more than twenty feet ahead of them. With that in mind, it was rather fortuitous that Garrison, Madeleine, Lulu, and Theo were enjoying a silent stretch when they turned the corner. Purple was all they had to see to know it was Munchauser. No one else wore purple suits in Massachusetts or, more aptly, all of New England.

After years on the field, Garrison's strategic instincts were well honed. He immediately crouched down behind one of the multitude of signs warning against entering the forest, signaling the others to follow suit. Munchauser's gnarled ugly face contorted with annoyance as he tried to pull Macaroni off the dirt shoulder. Clearly, he wasn't aware of the dog's distaste for the feel of cobblestone on his paws.

With one hand holding the leash, Munchauser dug deep into the leather satchel and pulled out a sandwich.

"Oh no," Theo whispered to Lulu. "What's he going to do to the sandwich?"

"You're worried about the sandwich? What is wrong with you?" Lulu responded.

"No, I was just wondering. Of course, I'm more worried about Macaroni . . . it was just a question."

"Shhh," Garrison hushed them as Munchauser attempted to lure Macaroni onto the road with the promise of a cheese sandwich.

"Lulu, Theo, you guys stay here. Maddie and I are going to cross the street. When I give you the signal, we're going to rush him. Try and get ahead of him so we can angle him against the forest."

"That's your best play? Rushing him? He's a giant purple monster and we're going to rush him?" Lulu asked with attitude.

"Do you have a better idea?" Garrison asked.

"Maybe," Lulu scoffed while Garrison held her gaze.

"Well?"

"Um, I'm thinking . . . we could . . . rush him," Lulu finally relented.

"That's what I thought," Garrison said with a smirk.

"That's what I thought," Lulu mimicked as Garrison and Madeleine crouched down to cross the road.

"Mimicking doesn't suit you, kind of like the color yellow," Theo whispered, to which Lulu could only roll her eyes.

Close to the forest's foliage, Madeleine instinctively began spraying. She was far too close to trees where insects, bugs, and spiders resided not to take every precaution available to her. Obviously, not all the creatures were gracious enough to come with a light on their backs; she needed to be ready for the covert operatives.

The sound of Madeleine's repellent was oddly familiar to Munchauser, prompting him to look up from Macaroni. Garrison threw himself on top of Madeleine, immediately drowning out the sound. As much as she loathed being stopped from dousing herself, this was the closest the two had come to hugging, and Madeleine rather enjoyed it. While she was always grateful for her veil, she was extraordinarily grateful in this moment, for it kept Garrison from seeing her crimson face.

"Five meatball sandwiches if you take one step onto this road. None of that kibble junk. I'm talking real ground beef; all you have to do is take one lousy step onto the road," Munchauser said through gritted teeth as he yanked at the dog's leash. "Do you know how many dogs would kill for ground beef? Do you? I bet you one million dollars you don't know how many dogs would kill for it. And don't worry, if you're wrong, I'll just take it out of your trust fund," Munchauser cackled to himself.

Garrison watched Munchauser closely, nervous that his feeble plan might not work. Lulu was right; it was hardly a very smart or cunning approach. On the other hand, it was the only plan they had. Garrison threw down his arm, signaling the others that it was time. Lulu and Theo took off first, attempting to get ahead of Munchauser on the road. Unfortunately, Theo's loud footsteps on the cobblestone immediately signaled their presence.

"Give us back our sandwich!" Theo screamed.

"Theo!" Lulu yelled.

"I mean dog! Give us back our dog!"

Garrison and Madeleine ran directly toward Munchauser, who was now attempting to lift the portly Macaroni. Theo and Lulu continued charging ahead as well. The plan appeared to have a chance at working when something tan, black, and furry descended en masse. It seemed that the flurry of running and yelling had disturbed a clan of squirrels. Almost straightaway, the squirrels went into battle mode, dive bombs and all. They courageously flung their bodies out of the trees, chattering loudly as they descended through the air.

Lulu was first to be hit, with one landing directly on

her face. Madeleine screamed with terror as two squirrels clung viciously to her veil with their teeth. As the
squirrels pulled, Madeleine fought hard. She had absolutely no intention of letting her veil go without a
brawl. It was only the arrival of a third and borderline
obese squirrel that proved more than she could handle.
The squirrels won, jumping to the ground with her
precious veil in their mouths. Within seconds, the
veil disappeared into the forest while Madeleine
stood dumbstruck.

Garrison managed to pull two squirrels from Theo's
back while removing a particularly determined one from
his own head. It was only after the squirrel mania had
died down that they realized Munchauser was gone.

CHAPTER 26

EVERYONE'S AFRAID OF SOMETHING:

Heliophobia is the fear of

the sun.

In his haste to escape, Munchauser dropped the sand-wich. There on the gray cobblestone lay a delicious cheese sandwich on thick sourdough bread. Theo, a true sandwich devotee, couldn't help but try to pick up the scrumptious item while running after Garrison. It was only Madeleine's reminder that stopped the boy from satiating his ever-growing hunger.

"Dirty fingernails, Theo! Years' worth of dirt!"

Madeleine hollered with her hands above her head, attempting to shield herself from the great outdoors.

Garrison and Lulu were first to turn the corner, spitting them out onto a long and equally foliage-enshrouded straightaway.

"Impossible! There's no way he could cover so much ground with a fifty-pound dog in his arms!" Garrison screamed while scanning the road ahead. There was nothing but green.

"Maybe he went into the forest?" Lulu added.

"I don't think so; if he was willing to brave that, he would have done it already."

Much like animals in the desert, Lulu and Garrison were moving slowly in an attempt to stalk their prey. Madeleine and Theo were oblivious companions, both terribly preoccupied with their own issues.

"Thank you so much, Madeleine," Theo whimpered. "I don't know what came over me. I'm not used to skipping breakfast, I guess. To think I could have ingested a sandwich that Munchauser had his dirty fingernails all over."

"Skipping a meal can be quite a shock to your system, kind of like losing your shadow," Madeleine said in reference to her veil.

Completely unaware of the emotional turmoil Madeleine was undergoing, Theo blabbered on. "Mad, will you be my sponsor on the trip? Stop me if I try to eat something dangerous or dirty or a meat product. I would hate to lose my many years of vegetarianism over —"

"Theo, look at my head! I've lost my veil. There's nothing between *me* and *them*," Madeleine said excitedly. "They could lay eggs in my hair! Or just drop them while flying by!"

"Give me your cans. I'm going to drench your head in so much repellent that your hair may actually fall out. You saved me, now I'm gonna save you."

"That's just great," Garrison said sarcastically, "but who's going to save Mac and Schmidty? How is it *possible* that a tall man in a purple suit carrying a fat bulldog can vanish without a trace?"

"Do you think it's unusual to develop arthritis in a day?" Theo asked as the glum foursome continued down the straightaway with no sign of Munchauser or Macaroni.

"'Cause my joints are really starting to hurt. I wish other people used this road; they could take me straight to the doctor. Not that I believe in hitchhiking, because normally I would never even consider getting into a stranger's car. But in this situation, I think I would revise my rules," Theo babbled on, seemingly unaware that no one was responding to him.

"Would you please stop talking?" Lulu interjected.

"Someone's being more than a little rude," Theo loudly whispered to Madeleine.

"I am not speaking to you, Theodore Bartholomew," Madeleine screeched with dripping wet hair.

"Mad, I said it was an accident! I had no idea your cans would run out. At least you can rest assured that no bugs or spiders will come within ten feet of your head."

"But what about the rest of me? My arms, legs, and face! They're completely open for attack! Look at me: no veil, no repellent on the front line of the war on spiders. Everywhere I turn it's nature, nature, and more nature, and everyone knows that spiders and insects live in nature!"

"I'm pretty sure you have repellent built up in your bloodstream. It will be years before a mosquito even comes near you," Lulu said.

Madeleine said nothing but quietly considered the merit of Lulu's statement.

"How long have we been walking? It feels like days since I've had any food or water."

"It's been two hours, Theo. Calm down," Lulu said.

"Two hours? That's it? That's only 120 minutes, 7,200 seconds."

"Thank you for the mathematical breakdown, Chubs. Definitely going to come in handy as we walk down a cobblestone road in the middle of nowhere!"

"No reason to bite my head off; I was merely commenting on how long we've been out here, braving the elements."

"You know what, Theo? It may have only been two hours, but if it makes you feel any better, your incessant whining has made it seem much longer. More like an entire day, which in case you didn't know is twenty-four hours, 1,440 minutes or . . ." Lulu paused trying to do the math in her head. ". . . a whole lot of seconds!"

"I see I'm not the only one who's feeling a little grumpy from lack of food."

"It's 86,400 seconds to be exact," Madeleine quietly mumbled to Garrison.

"You think this is grumpy? By the time we get to town you'll be smiling about the good old days before I gave you a black eye for talking too much!"

"Are you threatening me?" Theo asked with disdain.

"Maybe."

"I think I should tell you that anything you say can and will be used against you in a court of law."

"The Miranda rights," Madeleine said to Garrison, as if offering play-by-play commentary. It occurred so quickly and suddenly that it actually stopped Garrison's breath for a second. He was absolutely enchanted by Madeleine's bare face. In plain old thirteen-year-old boy speak, he thought she was cute.

"I'm not under arrest!" Lulu shot back at Theo.

"That phrase can be used at other times. Anyway, I just thought you should know that I am making a *mental note* of all your threats so that I can tell my mom and my lawyer once we get back."

"Would you stop? At the moment, you don't even have a cell phone, let alone a lawyer!"

"I may not have a lawyer right now, but this is a country where anyone can file a lawsuit, even a twelve-year-old. So get ready, Lulu Punchalower —"

"Wait!" Lulu interrupted Theo seriously. "Did someone just whimper?"

"You heard that, too?" Garrison responded, immediately on high alert.

Theo, Madeleine, Lulu, and Garrison froze, waiting to hear which direction the whimpering was coming from. It took a few seconds before they heard the muffled sound again. Lulu walked toward the forest's edge, eyes wide with a mixture of curiosity and anticipation. The recognition was sudden and jarring, but to her credit, she didn't scream.

"It's him."

"Who?" Garrison asked. "Munchauser?"

"Abernathy. I recognize him from the time I saw him peering in the dining room window," Lulu said while staring at Abernathy's thick and ashen face between the trees.

"And you waited until now to tell us," Theo admonished Lulu.

"I thought I'd imagined it . . . ," Lulu mumbled. "That face . . ."

Madeleine stepped behind Lulu, absolutely captivated by Abernathy's face.

Abernathy returned the children's stunned glare, never moving from just inside the forest's edge. The strange man knew that he was protected. No one, let alone children, would try to brave the dangers of the forest.

"Maybe we should say something? Offer him a snack or a drink of water," Theo said sincerely.

"Um, hello? In case you haven't noticed, we're not at the Four Seasons," Lulu snapped to Theo.

"Yeah, but by offering him something at least we're being polite. Maybe he'll warm up to us?"

Before anyone else could weigh in on the matter, Theo, making sure to speak loudly, launched the welcome wagon: "Hello! Hi, I'm Theo and this is Madeleine, Garrison, and Lulu. We're from the school on the hill; although, I think you may already know that since you've been spying on us, Mr. Abernathy. And by spying, I mean politely looking in the windows. Nothing wrong with that. We'd love to offer you some beverages or appetizers but we don't have any," Theo babbled on as Abernathy slowly moved his finger across his throat. Fortunately Theo was far too preoccupied by a strange noise to notice the intimidating gesture.

Now inches from the forest, Theo heard the whimper again and realized that it was far too close to be coming from Abernathy.

"Wait a minute," Theo said as he turned to his left, "you evil genius!"

Munchauser and Macaroni, covered head to toe in Greenland Fungus, were perfectly camouflaged against the forest's lush backdrop. Before anyone could mobilize, Munchauser tossed a mass of small yellow particles at the students. The smell was paralyzing, knocking all four students off their feet and to the ground. So rank and putrid was the stench that the foursome actually passed out. The last thing they remembered was the green silhouette of Munchauser and Mac taking off in the distance.

Madeleine was first to come to after the great tonsil stone battle. The smell was ripe, rancid, and overwhelmingly strong. She touched her face and realized that she had two stones glommed onto her cheek. Without hesitation, she ran to the forest's edge and began madly wiping her face with a leaf. So vile was the smell that she didn't even worry that insect eggs could be on the leaf.

"I think I'm going to die," Lulu moaned from the ground.

"Wipe your face!" Madeleine hollered, while remembering what Lulu said about having repellent in her blood. She prayed that it was true as she cleaned her face with a possible spider's home.

"Abernathy's gone," Garrison said as he surveyed the forest.

"Can you blame him? The smell. We need to move," Lulu said. "Garrison, drag Theo. He was hit the hardest. It may be days before he wakes up."

Garrison wiped Theo's face clean of tonsil stones while holding his breath. Luckily, Theo woke, overwhelmed by the olfactory purgatory.

"Help! The smell . . . the smell . . ."

"Come on, we gotta move," Garrison said firmly while pulling Theo to his feet.

The foursome jogged as fast as their sour stomachs would allow, keeping one eye open for suspicious green masses and the other for Abernathy.

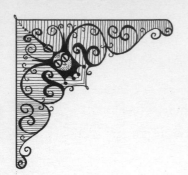

CHAPTER 27

EVERYONE'S AFRAID OF SOMETHING:

Cynophobia is the fear of

dogs.

The end of the forest came faster than Madeleine, Theo, Lulu, and Garrison had expected, releasing them into the powerful morning sunshine. The cobblestone road continued, surrounded by fields of tall grass with only the occasional tree. However lovely the sunshine felt on the foursome's faces, it also represented defeat to them.

In the dim light of the forest, retrieving Macaroni

still felt possible, even highly plausible. However, now as they carried on toward Farmington they felt the gap had grown too wide. By the time they reached town, Munchauser would probably have officially registered himself as Macaroni's guardian, leaving Schmidty in the cold. Garrison more than the others felt a particularly heavy burden, having been singled out by Schmidty to help him protect Macaroni.

Garrison led the moping brigade through curves, twists, and turns as they continued toward Farmington. While they were sure they had to be getting close to the small town, they hadn't seen any signs. So when Theo spotted a small brick house a few yards off the road, the group erupted in relief. Perhaps someone could drive them to town, giving them more than enough time to catch up with Munchauser.

Theo was thrilled at the concept of not only saving Macaroni but also eating something. He was beyond famished. In truth, he almost didn't say that he saw the brick house for fear that it was a hunger hallucination.

"I bet they have repellent!" Madeleine screamed with delight as she ran behind Theo.

"And sandwiches!"

"What joy, repellent and sandwiches," Lulu replied in her usual tone.

"Listen, guys, let me do the talking. We need to get to town as fast as possible, and I don't want us competing to tell a thousand different versions of the story."

Lulu, Madeleine, and Theo nodded as they approached the small brick house with blue shutters on it. Garrison leaped up the stairs to ring the doorbell next to the hand-painted sign that said THE KNAPPS. Theo and Madeleine busied themselves looking in the front window while Lulu joined Garrison on the porch.

A minute passed and no one came to the door. Garrison rang the bell again, praying for someone to answer. Another minute passed and still no one came to the door.

"I don't think anyone's home," Garrison called out to Theo and Madeleine.

At that moment, Madeleine did a very un-Madeleine-like thing. She stepped onto the flowerbed, crushing yellow tulips, and began banging on the glass window.

"We see you! We see you! Open this door right now! You ought to be ashamed of yourselves, hiding from small children in need of help! Absolutely shameful!"

Theo, who couldn't actually see anything from his position on the ground, joined in enthusiastically. He was never one to pass on theatrics.

"You people are rotten! We are sweet children in need of help! And sandwiches!"

On the floor of the living room, attempting to hide from the children, were a man and a woman in their early thirties. Dressed in similar preppy yellow sweaters, the smiling couple finally stood up and answered the door. By now Madeleine had pushed past Garrison, who was unsuccessfully trying to pick the lock on the front door, to tackle the role of group spokesperson.

"What kind of evil people hide from children?" Madeleine said while shoving the couple aside and stepping into the living room.

"Sorry about that, little lady; we thought you were orphans looking to find parents, and you see we really don't want any children," Mr. Knapp said awkwardly.

"Since when do orphans sell themselves door to door like Girl Scout cookies?" Madeleine huffed.

"Maddie, we don't have time for this. We need to get to town," Garrison explained calmly. "Look, we don't care why you didn't want to open the door. Can you drive us to town? It's sort of an emergency."

"We would love to help," Mrs. Knapp said cheerily.

"Thank you," Garrison said while breathing a sigh of relief.

"But we can't," she continued. "Our car has no gas in it."

"Thank heavens you don't have any children. What kind of irresponsible people let their car run out of gas?" Theo asked.

"Then let us use your phone," Garrison said with a desperate expression.

"Sorry, little lad," Mr. Knapp said, "can't do that either."

"I don't believe you," Garrison quickly retorted.

"Take a look for yourself," the man continued, pointing to the severed phone cords.

The cords were sliced neatly but were covered in grimy fingerprints. Almost immediately, Garrison knew Munchauser had been to the house. Rational people wouldn't sever their own phone lines.

"Did an ugly man and a large dog covered in green moss stop by here?" Garrison said seriously, completely ignoring the outrageous content of his statement.

"This is Massachusetts, not Mars," Mrs. Knapp said with an annoyingly chipper smile. "There aren't any green people here."

"Then who cut the phone cords?" Garrison prodded.

"I did," Mr. Knapp explained. "I felt we were becoming too dependent on talking to other people, so I cut the phone lines. Now if that's all, we really need to get back to talking to each other."

"You swear you haven't seen a man and a dog?" Garrison asked.

"Yes, we swear," Mrs. Knapp said with her default gregarious expression.

"Fine," Garrison said, defeated.

As the foursome turned to leave the strange couple's living room, Madeleine spotted something that simply was not right. A green cat.

"Why, you evil, despicable, lying people!" Madeleine railed into them. "I have half a mind to wash your mouths out with soap!"

322

"Maddie, what are you doing?" Garrison screamed at her.

"If they haven't seen Munchauser or Macaroni, why is their cat green?" Madeleine screamed, instantly sending Mrs. Knapp into waterworks.

"I'm sorry, that man threatened to kidnap our poodle Jeffrey if we didn't lie to you," Mr. Knapp explained. "He's in the bathroom with a really chunky bulldog and Jeffrey."

"Absolutely shameful," Madeleine continued.

"J-Jeffrey, our poodle," Mrs. Knapp blubbered, "he's like our child. I'm so sorry."

Through the living room window, Garrison spotted Munchauser, still covered in fungus, pulling Macaroni through a window into the backyard.

"There he is!" Garrison screamed while running for the back door.

"Don't let him hurt Jeffrey!" Mrs. Knapp screamed.

Madeleine, Theo, and Lulu took off after Garrison while the couple started for the bathroom, desperate to retrieve Jeffrey the poodle.

Munchauser ran as fast as possible with a big green

bulldog in his arms and nervously looking behind himself every few seconds. It was during one of those rearview moments when Munchauser discovered that his footing had drastically changed. The man was sinking. He had walked onto a pool covering. As the flimsy plastic cover ripped beneath the giant man's feet, he lost control of Macaroni, dropping him through the hole in the tarp. Ever the coward, with disaster near at hand, Munchauser continued to run, slightly faster now that he didn't have a bulldog in tow.

Garrison, closest to the pool, realized that Macaroni was drowning beneath the cover. Without thinking, he jumped through the hole and into the water. It wasn't a decision as much as it was a reaction. His instincts told him to save Macaroni, so that's what Garrison proceeded to do.

It wasn't until Garrison's body became submerged in the cool water that he remembered he couldn't swim. As he started to sink, Garrison spotted Macaroni doing the doggy paddle, quite literally. Of course as dogs are natural swimmers, Macaroni would be fine. He just needed someone to wipe the remaining moss from his face. Unfortunately, Garrison wouldn't be so lucky.

Garrison flailed violently, submerging much of the pool cover in his attempt to stay afloat. Theo nearly landed on top of Garrison when he heroically, but not gracefully, leaped to his friend's aid. He wrapped his arms around the gasping boy and deftly pulled him to the edge of the pool. Theo boosted Garrison up, and Lulu and Madeleine lifted him out of the water, as his now red face panted for air.

"It's okay, Garrison," Madeleine's said soothingly, "you're going to be just fine. We have you."

Garrison wanted to say thank you, but he couldn't speak; he was still coughing up pool water. So instead, he just looked at his friends and smiled.

"Gary's alive! Gary's alive!" Theo chanted happily.

"Just because you saved my life, doesn't mean you can call me Gary."

"Does Jeffrey really need to be in his car seat?" Lulu huffed as Mr. and Mrs. Knapp took a painstakingly long time to secure the furry brown poodle in his specially crafted canine seat belt.

"It's bad enough you made us wait to remove the fungus from his fur. We're losing precious time!" Garrison snapped with agitation.

"Would you let your baby ride in the car without a seat belt, knowing that any abrupt stop could send him flying through the windshield?" Mrs. Knapp said dramatically.

"If you like, we have an extra seat belt for your bulldog. It may be a little snug, but I think he can squeeze in there," Mr. Knapp said generously.

"We don't have time!" Garrison exploded. "We need to get to the sheriff."

"Do you know what the sheriff always says?" Mrs. Knapp asked Garrison with an annoyingly sincere smile.

"No," he relented under her well-brushed pearly whites.

"Buckle up, it's the law!"

"Yeah, for people! Not dogs!" Lulu jumped in.

"Maybe she's right," Theo blubbered. "I would hate to come this far and lose Mac in some silly traffic accident. Not to mention, he's pretty heavy. He could really hurt someone, flying through the car."

"Finally someone with a little common sense," Mrs. Knapp said with an undue amount of satisfaction. "Darling, go get the other seat belt," she instructed her husband before turning back to the children. "It will only take a second."

Mrs. Knapp greatly underestimated the level of difficulty and time required to shove a dog the size of a jumbo pumpkin into a car seat built for a dog with the dimensions of a cantaloupe. By the time Macaroni was fully buckled in, flab exploding from all sides, he looked more like an origami assignment gone wrong than a dog.

"Are you absolutely certain that the seat belt is helping Macaroni?" Madeleine asked. "He looks terribly uncomfortable."

"No one ever said safety was comfortable," Mrs. Knapp explained with a sigh.

"I've been saying that for years," Theo said while shaking his head.

Lulu and Theo surrounded Macaroni in the backseat while Madeleine and Garrison were forced to sit in the far back of the Knapps' Suburban. Not surprisingly Jeffrey sat between the Knapps in the front seat. Mrs. Knapp hand-fed the poodle bits of cheese, which she refused to share with Theo, as Mr. Knapp pulled out of the driveway.

"What are you doing?" Lulu hollered from the backseat. "You're turning the wrong way."

"No, I'm not. I've lived here seven years; I should know which way town is," Mr. Knapp said confidently.

"Actually, darling," Mrs. Knapp said softly, "I think she's right."

"No, darling, I'm right," Mr. Knapp said aggressively.

"But the forest's ahead," Mrs. Knapp continued.

"Why am I never right?" Mr. Knapp huffed while banging his fists on the steering wheel.

As Mr. Knapp started the laborious forty-seven-point turn necessary to turn around, the car remained utterly silent. Well, except for Macaroni's light growls of discomfort.

"So was that a rhetorical question?" Theo said to Mr. Knapp. "Or do you actually want to know why you're never right? 'Cause I have some ideas."

The cold stare in the rearview mirror said it all. Theo nodded while silently planning to campaign for the elimination of rhetorical questions at school this fall. They seemed to cause a lot of problems.

By the time the Suburban pulled up in front of the sheriff's office in Farmington, Macaroni resembled a bulging pretzel. Never had a dog been so happy to get out of a car. After all he had been through that day, one got the feeling that the ten-minute car ride was the most painful.

"Should we wait for you?" Mr. Knapp offered the foursome as they slammed the back door shut.

"Absolutely not," Lulu answered first.

"And she means that in the most gracious way possible," Madeleine added. "We know you must be anxious to get Jeffrey back home."

"Well, I am a bit concerned that Jeffrey's showing signs of" — Mrs. Knapp stopped to cover Jeffrey's ears and whispered — "low self-esteem on account of Munchauser passing him over for a bulldog, of all breeds."

As the Suburban rolled away, Mrs. Knapp grabbed Jeffrey's paw and waved goodbye to the foursome.

The children waved back obligingly, when Lulu could have sworn she saw Macaroni roll his eyes.

CHAPTER 28

EVERYONE'S AFRAID OF SOMETHING:

Phobophobia is the fear

of phobias.

W hen four kids with wet, dirty, stained, and smelly clothes stormed into Sheriff McAllister's office with Mrs. Wellington's dog, he wondered if his wife was pulling a joke on him.

"What on Earth?"

"Mrs. Wellington died and she left everything to Macaroni because she thought Schmidty would be dead, but of course he's not, so Munchauser, her attorney, stole Macaroni and we had to chase him down. We got

Macaroni back, but we didn't catch Munchauser," Theo blurted out rapidly.

"Did you just say Mrs. Wellington is dead?" the sheriff said with his eyes misting up.

"Yes, I'm afraid we did," Madeleine said calmly.

"I've known her since I was a young boy. Why, she was the one who got me over my fear of flying," the sheriff said as he dabbed his eyes with a tissue. "I used to take the *Queen Mary* to see my Great Aunt Melba in Liverpool. And I'd get so seasick on the ship, but then Mrs. Wellington stepped in, changing my life and my posture."

"Listen, Sheriff, I want to come back to that story of how she helped you, I really do, but right now we need to get back to Summerstone. I'm worried about Schmidty," Garrison said sadly.

"Don't you worry, son. I'll get the van," the sheriff said while putting on his hat.

"The crane's broken," Lulu said. "Schmidty said Munchauser broke it."

"Which means we'll have to take the tunnel," Garrison said with defeat. "Again."

"I don't think so," the sheriff said confidently as he walked toward the door.

The sheriff managed to coax Farmington's fire captain, Huckleford, into driving the group out to the base of Summerstone. The truck's ladder extended almost two hundred and twenty-five feet, allowing the group to bypass the dreaded tunnels.

While Captain Huckleford drove, the students stared out the windows, contemplating all that had happened. Though less than a week had passed, the children felt that years' worth of experiences had transpired since they left their families. And never in their wildest dreams or even nightmares had any of them expected to weather an adventure like the one they had just completed.

After what felt like an eternity, the fire truck arrived at the base of the granite plateau. Captain Huckleford called everyone on deck and began extending the mechanical ladder.

"The sheriff's going up to make sure Schmidty's okay," Captain Huckleford explained to the kids.

"We're going, too," Theo said with sweaty palms.

"It's awfully high; are you sure you want to do that?" Captain Huckleford asked.

"We're sure," Theo said boldly for the group.

Theo, Madeleine, Lulu, Garrison, and the sheriff scaled the ladder with surprising ease and speed. However, as soon as they reached the top, Theo looked down and began to feel faint.

"I think I'll take the tunnel down, if you don't mind," Theo whispered to the others.

"Come on!" the sheriff yelled while barreling toward Summerstone.

The second they entered the foyer, the group began screaming Schmidty's name.

"Schmidty! Schmidty!"

"Where are you?"

"Hello? Hello? Schmidty?"

A small voice managed to be heard in all the bedlam.

"I'm in the dining room." Schmidty's voice was weaker than usual, certainly not a good sign.

They ran past familiar doors from the clock to the brass doorknob before stopping in front of the chalkboard door that led to the dining room. As the sheriff went to open the door, Garrison pushed in front of him, entering the room first. Lulu, Madeleine, Theo, and finally the sheriff quickly followed.

Seated at the elaborately set table were Mrs. Wellington, Schmidty, and Munchauser. As the foursome stood in absolute shock, the sheriff laughed and took a seat at the table.

Theo was first to approach Mrs. Wellington, reaching his small hand to her makeup-clad face.

"Are you really alive?" Theo asked sincerely.

"Yes, Theo, I am," Mrs. Wellington replied sweetly.

Theo flung his arms around her neck before planting a kiss on her cheek. "I have so many things I want to ask you, but first, do you have any idea what you put us through, woman?"

"Not only are you not dead, but you are eating with the enemy!" Lulu screamed while pointing to Munchauser.

"Someone better start talking," Garrison said, attempting to remain calm.

"Congratulations, you've completed School of Fear," Mrs. Wellington said in her usual formal tone. "And with flying colors, I might add. We are all extremely proud."

"I'm terribly confused and very upset," Madeleine said. "I'm feeling a little overwhelmed by my emotions."

"So it was all fake?" Theo lamented angrily. "This whole thing was one big elaborate setup?"

"Well, not exactly. Munchauser's arrival was not planned. But with Abernathy in the forest, I decided it best to improvise so he could accompany you into town. This was Munchauser's first time taking part in an adventure; we usually try to keep him away from the students for obvious reasons. He doesn't have the best bedside manner, and as you may have noticed, he has a fondness for gambling."

"I didn't think any of you would make it. I bet Schmidty one dollar and lost," Munchauser grumbled rudely. "Anyone got a dollar I could borrow?"

"I almost died in that tunnel, Mrs. Wellington," Lulu said angrily, "do you realize that?"

"Not to worry, Lulu. We watched the whole thing, each step of the adventure, on closed circuit televisions. Every inch of the tunnels and road, even the Knapps' house, is monitored by cameras."

"Garrison would have died in that pool if not for *my* heroic save," Theo said proudly to Mrs. Wellington.

"The Knapps are certified lifeguards, my swimming sausage. He was never in any actual peril."

"But what if we had gone into the forest?" Madeleine asked. "We could have really been hurt."

"Oh my former little beekeeper, if any of you had actually started to enter the forest, I would have used the speaker system to stop you."

"And Abernathy?" Lulu asked suspiciously. "He was also in on this?"

"I'm afraid," Mrs. Wellington said with shame, "that part of the story is true. He is my one failure and such a painful one at that."

As Mrs. Wellington squirmed at the mention of Abernathy, Theo approached with a serious expression.

"Does this mean we can finally go home? Or do we still have to stay here for the rest of the summer?"

"Your families are expecting you home tomorrow. You will return braver and infinitely stronger. They will be so proud that you overcame your fears."

"Not to disappoint you, but I'm still kind of afraid of death. Just a little," Theo whispered, "only a smidge."

"And I'm still not terribly keen on spiders," Madeleine added.

"It's a process, contestants; a process of constantly challenging yourselves. Now that you've taken your first steps here, you will continue to make progress each summer, and soon you won't even remember a time when you had such phobias."

"Excuse me, Mrs. Wellington, but did you just say 'each summer'?" Madeleine asked.

"Of course, I did, Madeleine. I'm sure you all read the fine print on the brochure about the program."

The stunned foursome was far too exhausted to respond to the information they had just learned, and after such an emotional day they could barely think of going through such a harrowing experience again.

"Everyone please take a seat, the food is getting cold," Schmidty instructed the group.

"Fiona, Errol, Annabelle, Ratty," Mrs. Wellington called to the cats, "the contestants need to wash their hands."

The four cats trotted into the room, in black-gray-black-gray formation. One by one, they each jumped onto the table, and dropped a steaming hot napkin on each child's place setting.

"So they really *are* trained?" Theo said incredulously.

"Well *of course* they're trained," Mrs. Wellington

said smugly. "Don't tell me after all this, you still under-estimate me."

The foursome stared intently at Mrs. Wellington, assessing the many facets of the peculiar woman.

"You really are diabolically smart," Lulu said with overt admiration.

"Thank you," Mrs. Wellington said with a knowing nod.

"And your determination, it's absolutely impenetrable," Madeleine added with blossoming awe.

"It feels sort of weird to say this, but you totally know what you're doing," Garrison said with surprise.

"Thank you, Sporty." Mrs. Wellington then turned expectantly to Theo.

"I think you should seriously reconsider letting Schmidty do your makeup."

"Theo!" Madeleine, Lulu, and Garrison screamed as Mrs. Wellington's lips turned fire-engine red before breaking into a wry smile.

"Perhaps you're right, my portly friend."

Keep reading for a sneak peek of

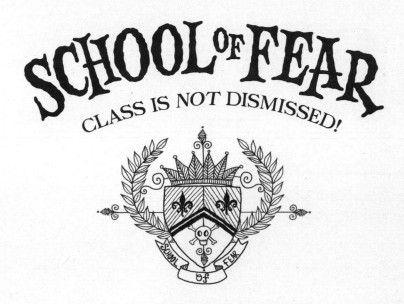

SCHOOL ᴼᶠ FEAR

CLASS IS NOT DISMISSED!

SCHOOL OF FEAR

The wilderness outside Farmington, Massachusetts
(Exact location withheld for security purposes)
Direct all correspondence to: PO Box 333, Farmington, MA 01201

Dear Contestants,

Much like homework, pimples, and puberty, your second summer at School of Fear is not optional. Any acts of insubordination such as death of a beloved pet, amnesia, or enrollment in sleepaway camp will be met by my lawyer Munchauser—quite literally. The man with the dirtiest fingernails in all of America shall arrive at your home with dental floss in hand. Munchauser, who has only thrice been to a dentist, shall then proceed to floss his small yellow teeth mere inches from your face. This is an act from which you will not recover.

The summer course shall begin promptly at 9:00 AM on Saturday May 29th at the base of Summerstone. And do remember to guard School of Fear's anonymity by running the bath, blaring the television, and playing the harmonica whenever discussing our institution. On behalf of myself, my comb-over-clad assistant Schmidty, Macaroni the bulldog, and my highly trained cats, we look forward to seeing all of your Vaseline-coated smiles terribly soon.

Fondest regards,

Mrs. Wellington

MRS. WELLINGTON
Headmistress, School of Fear
49-Time Pageant Winner

P.S. Munchauser is not the slightest bit interested in seeing any of you again, and requested that I tell you all as much.

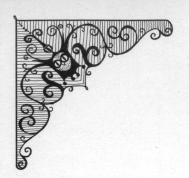

CHAPTER 1

EVERYONE'S AFRAID OF SOMETHING:

Heliophobia is the fear

of the sun.

The sun is not the sun. And that isn't to say that the sun is the moon, for that is most definitely not the case. The sun is simply far more than the center of the solar system or a bright shiny thing in the sky. Day after day the sun wrestles us from darkness, bringing with it the many secrets we hide from others and occasionally even ourselves. Oh yes, the sun is the guardian of truth, whether we like it or not.

Thirteen-year-old Madeleine Masterson breezed into

Boston, utterly delighted to have escaped the dreary skies of London. With a beaming smile the fair-skinned, blue-eyed girl with raven locks just shy of her shoulders led her parents into the blazing heat and humidity. The entire Masterson family stood outside warming their chilly British bones in the extraordinary sunshine. For the English, the sun is a bit like the Queen; they know she exists but they simply don't see her that often.

Only a year earlier, Madeleine had been a shell of her current self, walking through life in abject terror, certain that enemies lurked around every corner, or rather *in* every corner. Mr. and Mrs. Masterson's only child had long suffered from a dreadful phobia of spiders and other insects. In addition to wearing a netted veil and a belt of repellents at all times, Madeleine had refused to enter any building that had not been fumigated recently by an exterminator. As one might imagine, most of her classmates' parents refused to meet the extensive and expensive guidelines necessary before Madeleine could enter their residences. Thus Madeleine missed out on slumber parties, birthdays, and all outdoor activities.

Most fortunately for all involved, Madeleine had spent the previous summer at the highly clandestine, word-of-mouth institution known as School of Fear. Much to her parents' delight, Madeleine had returned veil- and repellent-free, an absolutely changed child. Well, not entirely changed; the young girl remained fascinated by world leaders, often listing United Nations delegates in alphabetical order for entertainment. But long gone was her crippling arachnophobia.

"Mummy and Daddy, not to be impertinent, but why are you sending me back for another summer? I'm cured, fixed, or however you care to put it. Might I remind you that I am now a member of the Spider Appreciation Club as well as Eight-Legged Creatures for Social Change?"

"Yes, we know, dear. Your father and I are both terribly impressed with your progress," Mrs. Masterson said with a smile.

"Aren't you the only member of those clubs?" Mr. Masterson inquired.

"That is hardly the point, Daddy," Madeleine replied huffily.

"Unfortunately, as we've explained, it's a contractual issue. Mrs. Wellington's attorney, that ghastly man Munchauser, had us sign a two-summer agreement. He claims the second session is necessary to reinforce the progress you made last summer. But not to worry, dear. Next summer you will be free to do anything you like."

"Well, I suppose another summer won't hurt me too badly. Plus I am terribly keen to see the others again and have a proper catch-up," Madeleine acquiesced as the town car turned onto a narrow cobblestone road. Within seconds the car was shrouded in darkness cast by the trees and sticky vines that grew from one side of the road to the other, creating a tunnel. Although hard to decipher in the faint light, a multitude of homemade signs warned against entering the Lost Forest. The densely wooded area had quite the reputation for chewing people up and *not* spitting them out.

The car slowed as the foliage tunnel opened at the base of a large granite mountain. Mr. and Mrs. Masterson had planned to exit the vehicle and meet this Schmidty character they had heard so much about. However, the soaring temperatures quickly dissuaded the London natives from leaving the air-conditioned confines of their car. Sporting an orange tartan dress with a matching headband, with a massive grin Madeleine bounded out of the sedan. Technically speaking, it was more of a saunter than a bound, due to the blistering weather. Madeleine was beginning to understand what people meant by too much of a good thing.

Seated on lawn chairs under a large umbrella were Schmidty, School of Fear's trusty cook/groundskeeper/ wig groomer, and Macaroni, the English bulldog.

"Schmidty!" Madeleine yelped joyfully, before stopping. The young girl was utterly gobsmacked and unable to speak. The plump old man was dressed in a Hawaiian shirt, polyester black shorts, and open-toed sandals that showcased his furry feet and jagged brown toenails. But most offensive was the sight of his fallen comb-over; a mess of gray ringlets was all that remained. Madeleine stared for a few seconds before regaining her composure and assessing how best to handle the delicate situation.

"Schmidty, I'm awfully sorry to inform you, but your hair—"

"Please, Miss Madeleine," Schmidty interrupted, "it's too painful to hear confirmation. I'm attempting a state of denial, but you know it's much harder than Mrs. Wellington makes it look."

Madeleine nodded in agreement before patting Schmidty on the shoulder. In light of the heat and the fallen comb-over, Madeleine thought it best to avoid a hug.